A challenge for the throne . . .

A horn blew far off in the field beyond the castle, and a small party of mounted men rode up the hill toward Doun. One of them carried the banner of Hugo de la Corre—a huge raven, its wings outstretched in flight. Another wore the blank white surcoat of a herald. They rode up to the limits of the magic circle. The invisible boundary flared up briefly with blue light when the lead horse touched it. The creature reared, and refused to go farther.

"All you in the castle," the herald called. "If you will surrender the girl and swear fealty to King Hugo, we will depart in peace."

Diamante stepped forward before Lord Alyen could speak. She mounted up onto the parapet, where all those below could see her, and stood with her long silver hair unbound and whipping out behind her like a banner in the wind.

"If the pretender desires peace, let him go back to his own lands," she cried, in a voice that carried over tower and field. "But I am the true and rightful queen, and it is *you* who must swear allegiance to *me*."

CIRCLE OF MAGIC

THE

HIGH KING'S DAUGHTER

Debra Doyle and James D. Macdonald

illustrated by Judith Mitchell

Troll

For Ellen Steiber, editor *sans peur et sans reproche*.

I.
Borderlands

A GUST OF wind blew in through the doorway of the abandoned hut, driving the stinging rain before it. The fire on the stone hearth fizzled and went out in a thin trail of gray smoke. Randal of Doun sighed, pulled up the hood of his wizard's robe to protect himself against the cold and wet, and started to remake the fire. Carefully, he laid the kindling in place, then held his hands over the arrangement of sticks and tinder and murmured the words of fire-starting.

For a moment nothing happened, even though Randal felt the peculiar mental *snap*—once experienced, never forgotten—that told him the spell had worked. Then, without warning, the sticks and tinder ignited in a flash, sending a tongue of orange flame reaching up to lick at his sleeves. He jerked his hands away from the hearth and sat back on his heels, watching as the fire began to fill the hut with hazy smoke.

The closer we get to Elfland, he thought, *the more*

unreliable our human magic becomes. It shouldn't have taken me more than one try to start a fire like that, even with the wind against me. I've known that spell since I was an apprentice.

The interior of the hut darkened briefly as Randal's cousin, Sir Walter—Randal's senior by four years and, at the age of twenty, already a knight—stooped to come in through the low doorway.

"Only one day's worth of food in our saddlebags." The knight's breath made a gray cloud in front of his lips as he spoke. "I hope Master Madoc finds the gateway before our rations give out."

Randal paused in his task of feeding more kindling to the fire and looked up at his cousin. "It won't be long now," he said. "I can feel it."

"I hope you're right," said Walter. He sat down on the dirt floor near the fire and held out his hands to the flames. Faint wisps of steam rose from the sodden wool of his cloak. "It's late autumn already. Once the snow falls and the passes close, we'll be stuck here without provisions until spring."

Randal shook his head. "Once we find the gateway into Elfland, earthly food and drink are no good anyway. I know that much. Where are Lys and Madoc?"

"There's a spring nearby, Madoc says," Walter replied. "They went off looking for it while I tended to the horses. Lys was going to bring back some water, and Madoc . . . I'm not sure what he was planning to do. He said something about talking to the hills and listening to the wind, whatever that means."

"It means we're close to the gateway," said Randal. For a while, he sat watching the wisps of smoke that curled up from the fire. Then he looked up. "You've come this far," he said to his cousin. "All the long road from Bell Castle . . . There's still time for you to turn back before we reach the gate. I'm the only one who needs to go through."

"I gave you my word," said Walter. "Do you really think I'd abandon a friend and a kinsman at a time like this?"

"No," Randal said. "But I had to ask. Something tells me that bringing the High King's daughter out of Elfland isn't going to be as simple as it sounds."

Walter laughed. "Don't fool yourself, cousin. Nothing about this quest of ours is going to be simple. You can worry about getting the princess home to Brecelande. I'll worry about what comes after."

"What do you mean?"

"I mean," said Walter, "that setting the princess on her father's throne is likely to make storming the gates of Elfland look easy. Brecelande's been without a ruler these twenty years and more, ever since the High King died and the princess vanished. The great lords have grown used to doing as they please, with no true monarch to hold them back, while the common folk turn to outlawry out of greed and fear. And look at the three of us —a knight errant, a foreign minstrel, and a journeyman wizard. Not what I'd pick to pull order out of chaos, or make the earls swear fealty to an unknown girl."

Another gust of wind blew more rain into the hut. Raindrops hissed on the hot coals, but this time the fire kept on burning. Randal pulled his robe tighter around him and huddled closer to the hearth.

"I know," he said, rubbing his hands together to work some life back into flesh gone stiff with cold. In chilly, wet weather like this, the ugly scar running across his right palm ached unmercifully: a perpetual reminder that some actions have lifelong consequences. "But we have to try. All our lives, Brecelande's had nothing but wars and struggles for power. We've been lucky so far—Doun is well-guarded and prosperous, and the Schola protects Tarnsberg—but it's only a matter of time before the troubles touch them, too. And I still have my studies to complete, if I'm ever to become a master wizard myself."

As he finished speaking, Lys's slight, dark-haired figure appeared in the doorway of the hut. The young Occitanian minstrel was dressed in boy's clothing—her usual custom on the road. In one hand she carried a goatskin water-bag and in the other a lute in a leather case.

She hung the waterskin from a stub on one of

4

the low, rough-hewn rafters, then sat down beside Randal and took out her lute. The strings jangled as she ran her fingers across them. She frowned and began the task of bringing them back into tune.

"He's right, Walter," she said quietly to the knight as she plucked first one string and then another. "Believe me, I know. If there's anything that might keep the fighting away from your home and family, then it's worth a try."

She fell silent, her blue eyes darkened by memories, and Randal knew she was thinking about her own family—a troupe of traveling players from the far south, attacked and murdered by the bandits that infested the rulerless kingdom of Brecelande.

For a while, nobody said anything. The strings of the lute sounded one at a time under Lys's fingers, single notes repeating over and over as they gradually came into agreement. The girl began to sing, a melancholy tune that seemed to drift upward along with the smoke from the fire and lose itself somewhere among the rafters.

"Home, home, home, gladly would I be,
Home, home, home, in my own country,
For the oak and the ash and the bonny
    rowan tree,
They all flourish green in my own country."

Outside the hut, the gray light slowly faded,

making the doorway into a low rectangle of black. The wind gusted and howled. Finally, footsteps sounded on the threshold, and Randal looked up from the fire to see Madoc the Wayfarer as he entered the hut. The master wizard's dark-brown hair and close-trimmed beard were soaked with rain, and drops of water fell from the edges of his saffron tunic and his kilted cloak of gray wool. He looked exhausted, as though he came from long hours of backbreaking labor, or from time spent in difficult and powerful conjurations.

"The gateway to Elfland is only a short ride from here," he said to Randal as he joined the others around the hearth. "Once the sun is up, I can guide you that far, but no farther. I left the Fair Realm once before, of my own will, and no man or woman who does that can ever return."

Randal poked at the fire with a twig and watched the sparks follow the smoke-trails upward. "What's it like?" he asked. "Elfland, I mean. All I know is what the masters told us at the Schola: that elves and demons live on planes of existence outside our own, where time and place have no meaning. I've never had any dealings with the elfin plane, but I've met demons before . . . and if elves are anything like them—"

Madoc gave a weary chuckle. "Hardly, lad. And don't make that suggestion where someone from the Fair Realm can hear you . . . they might not see the joke."

Lys ran her fingers across the strings of the lute

in a faint, questioning chord. "The songs and stories all talk about the dangers of Elfland," she said. "Are you saying they lied?"

Madoc shook his head. "They spoke the truth as they knew it," he told her. "The Erlking—the King of all the Elves—rules over a land wondrous to visit, but perilous, as well. The greatest danger is that you may never wish to leave."

"Is it that beautiful?" asked Walter curiously.

"Beauty is the least of it," said the master wizard, a note of sadness coming into his voice, "though the Erlking's land is not called the Fair Realm as an idle compliment. But all those things that time can touch, all those things that here in this human world will someday rust or decay or fall from their prime—in Elfland, these same things will last forever in perfect condition. Swords that never rust, musical instruments that never lose their tune, trees that bear fruit, blossoms, and green spring leaves on the same branch . . . and magic of power and subtlety beyond human measure."

The master wizard sighed. "I wished never to leave there, but leave I did. After I'd brought the High King's daughter to safety among the elves, I came back to Brecelande to help him fight his enemies. But time passes strangely in the Fair Realm, and when I reached the mortal world, I found my friend already dead and buried."

Lys looked up from her lute. "I've heard tales like that about travelers spending years in Elfland when it seemed to them a single night," she said.

7

"And other stories, too—is it true that you should never eat or drink there?"

Madoc half-smiled. "You'll get very hungry and thirsty if you don't," he replied. "The fruits of Elfland aren't poison, and eating them won't keep you a prisoner there forever. But all those who taste them are changed."

The wizard fell silent. Lys went on playing—haunting, dying notes and minor chords, an echo of Randal's mood. The night grew darker, the fire burned low, and at last the four travelers fell into a cold and uncomfortable sleep.

A gray morning dawned. In silence, the four companions saddled and mounted the horses that had carried them north from the siege of Bell Castle. After riding for some hours, they ascended over a low ridge of hills and looked down on a slate-colored sea, stretching in an unbroken line to the northern horizon. For days they had ridden over rocky and broken ground covered with gorse and heather, but here the grass grew lush and green on the shore. Silver birch trees stretched all the way down to the water's edge.

Walter reined in his horse at the top of the rise. "I mistrust this place," he said to Madoc. "We haven't seen trees and grass like this for weeks, and there was no smell of salt in the air last night or this morning."

"This is the gateway into Elfland," Madoc told him. "Will you come with me?"

Walter started his horse trotting forward. "If this is the road by which we can bring peace and plenty to Brecelande," said the knight, "then nothing will hold me back."

Randal spurred his horse forward to ride even with his cousin's. Lys and Madoc came up more slowly behind them, and all four started into the birches that stood between the meadow and the sea. They had been riding through the slender white trees for some minutes before Randal noticed that the birch thicket stretched out farther than it should have.

"I hear the ocean ahead of us," he said. "When will we reach it?"

"It isn't far now," Madoc replied.

Randal saw that he spoke the truth. Under the cloudy sky, the trees ended abruptly at the edge of the water. "Continue straight on from here," Madoc said. "I can go no farther."

Randal, Walter, and Lys urged their horses forward into the stream. The water came up to the horses' bellies, then higher. Randal heard a cry from Lys.

"The water . . . it's warm!"

They reined in their horses and sat looking down at the water. It was salty, as Randal had expected, but where the ocean they had seen from the shore was a dull lead, here the water flowed as clear and sparkling as crystal over pure white sand. The fish that darted back and forth in the current had bright scales of red and blue and yellow.

"I've seen the waters of the south," said Walter to Randal, "and sailed the seas of the western isles, but I've never seen an ocean like this. What kind of place have you brought us to?"

Randal, who had seen the ocean at Tarnsberg and Widsegard, could only shake his head and look to Madoc still waiting behind them.

"The rivers that feed this sea do not spring in mortal lands," the master wizard replied from the shore. "Carry on, and be of good heart, for you have reached the border between the Fair Realm and our own." Then he turned his horse and disappeared among the trees.

"Let's go," said Randal at last. He rode forward, and the others followed.

As they made their way through the water, the strange sea never grew shallower, but at least it never grew deeper. Before long, the birch trees vanished behind them, and no farther shore appeared. The air hung motionless and heavy, and low gray clouds hid the location of the sun—if any sun still shone.

Then a dark line appeared on the horizon ahead of them. The darkness grew closer as they rode on, until it became a bank of land looming gray and mossy above them. Randal saw that they were riding toward the farther shore. They urged their horses onward and scrambled up the bank, going from shadow into sunlight as they rode. The last of the clouds burned away as they reached the top of the bank, and they stood on emerald-green grass beneath a sky of clear, perfect sapphire blue.

Randal turned in his saddle to look back at the way they had come. He swallowed a cry of surprise. The water had vanished, and the field on which they now stood stretched all the way back to the southern horizon.

Was that really the gateway? he wondered. *If it was, then it's true that elfin magic works differently from the magic wizards know.*

His cousin interrupted his thoughts. "All right, Randy—which way should we go now?"

Randal turned back and saw Walter pointing at the land ahead of them, where three paths led out across the gently rolling hills. On the right-hand side, a narrow path headed sharply uphill; it was blocked by boulders and sharp rocks, and bushes and brambles with long thorns hemmed it closely on either side.

"If we went that way," said Walter, "it would be slow, and we'd have to ride in single file. But if I were by myself, that's the path I'd choose—one man alone could hold it against many."

To the left, a pair of upright stones marked the beginning of a long path that was broad and level and led to the horizon. Lys looked at it and shivered.

"Those stones remind me of teeth," she said, "and it gives me a bad feeling. We could travel fast on a track like that—but I think that somebody chasing us could travel even faster."

Directly in front of them ran the third road,

marked only by the deeper color of the grass as it meandered between the gentle hills.

"I say we take the middle road," said Randal after a moment's thought. "It doesn't seem either too easy or too hard, and it's more pleasing to look at than either of the others. This is the Fair Realm, after all."

They rode on under a blue sky dappled with high white clouds. The air smelled sweet and clean, and a warm breeze ruffled the taller grass to either side of the road. At length, just as the sun was setting, they came to a single tree standing on top of a low hill. Ahead of them, the darker green of the road wound farther northward among the grassy hills.

The three companions paused on the hilltop beside the tree. Globes of golden fruit hung from its branches. Beneath it sat a dark-haired young woman in a dress of grass-green velvet, absorbed in her task of threading glass beads on a cord. Her hands were long and slender, and moved with a swift, accurate grace. Her hair was unbound and flowed back from her smooth white brow. She might almost have been human, Randal thought, except that her features had an uncanny loveliness, a kind of carved-ivory perfection not marred by any spot or blemish—a beauty, such as Master Madoc had told of, that time would never touch.

The elf-maid set aside her handiwork and stood to greet the three. She spoke musical words that Randal couldn't quite understand and held out a carved wooden bowl full of the golden fruit.

"I believe she wants us to have them," said the young wizard. "And if we want to be guests here in Elfland, I don't think we should refuse."

He bent down in his saddle and took one of the fruits. Lys took another, and then, after a moment's hesitation, so did Walter. The young woman in green took the last fruit, raised it to her lips, and took a bite.

Again Walter looked at Randal. "What now?"

Randal weighed the fruit on the palm of his hand. The golden sphere felt ripe and bursting with juice. After weeks of nothing but trail rations, his mouth watered at the fragrance—a rich, heady scent, like honey and spices mingled together.

"Madoc said that the fruits of Elfland would neither kill us nor imprison us," he said at last. "And I'm willing to chance whatever else may happen."

He bit into the fruit. The yellow flesh was soft and sweet, and the sticky juice ran down over his chin. Then he raised his eyes. The hills, which before had seemed covered only with blowing grass and wildflowers, were now dotted with small cottages; a castle rose in the distance, glistening with crystal and gold.

"Welcome to Elfland," said the young woman, her smile both friendly and triumphant. "We have long awaited your coming. The Erlking expects you."

II.

In the Erlking's Hall

"DISMOUNT AND FOLLOW ME," the elf-maid said. "You have no need to ride. Your steeds will be well provided for, and it is pleasant to walk in these parts."

Randal was aware of Lys and Walter watching him and waiting. It made the young wizard uneasy to know that his older cousin—who'd always, without question, taken the lead during their boyhood days at Castle Doun—now looked to him for guidance. He gave an inward shrug. *You should know by now that if Walter's going to trust your judgment, he's going to trust it completely. Now decide.*

He flung the pit of the fruit aside into the grass and dismounted. Behind him he heard the jingle of metal and the creak of leather as Lys and Walter did the same.

"Come with me," the elf-maid said again as she started down the slope toward the castle of gold and crystal. Randal and the others followed, leading their horses.

All along the way, Randal saw strange flowers blooming beside the path: unearthly blossoms with delicate, luminous petals of white and gold. A sweet smell drifted upward from their centers, but it was the sickly sweetness of meat that had lain too long uncooked.

He frowned. *Master Madoc didn't mention anything like this.* He glanced over his shoulder at Lys and Walter, but the knight and the lute-player seemed not to notice anything wrong with the flowers.

Randal shook his head and continued to walk behind their guide. At length, they drew near the castle. The fanciful golden towers suddenly appeared dull, as if covered with a thin layer of soot, and the glass windows that had caught the light from far off were dirty and cracked.

Something's wrong, Randal thought as he and the others followed the elf-maid through the open gates. *This isn't the land of unchanging beauty that Madoc told us about.*

Their guide took them to a suite of rooms in a tower by the gatehouse. "Refresh yourselves," she said, "and make yourselves welcome. You may come and go as you please, so long as you are in the great hall when the horn blows and the feast begins. The Erlking will be greatly disappointed if you are not there."

With that, she curtsied low and departed. The three friends separated and went to the chambers assigned to them. Alone in his room, Randal washed himself clean of the dust of travel in water from a crystal basin. The cool air striking his damp skin made him shiver, although a fire burned in the chamber fireplace. He approached the hearth curiously and found that the flames gave no heat.

Randal wondered if they were illusions. *If this is the magic of Elfland,* he thought, *then Master Madoc spoke of it too kindly. Any mortal wizard could do the same and take more care with the details.*

He walked away from the fireplace, picked up a silver goblet from his bedside table, and turned it over in his hands. As he'd expected, dark smudges of tarnish blackened the curves and whorls of the cup's design. He put the cup aside and turned to the fresh clothing laid out for him on the bed.

After he'd put on the clean tunic and hose and the soft leather boots, he reached for his journeyman's robe. The sturdy woolen robe had been new when he left the city-state of Peda in the far south, but it had gone through hard traveling since then. Now, to his surprise, the robe that met his hand was made of black velvet lined with silk. A closer look showed that it was sewn together in one piece without either stitch or needlework.

It seems that there are still a few marvels left in Elfland, he thought. He hesitated a moment and then adjusted the rich garment into place with a shrug of his shoulders. He left his chamber and joined the others in the castle courtyard. Walter wore a silken surcoat over a gleaming coat of mail, and Lys was clothed in a tunic and hose of deep-green satin embroidered with gold thread. They

16

stood for a little while, regarding one another in silence.

Finally, Lys turned to Randal and said, "What now?"

"I think that we should find the princess and leave as soon as possible," he said. "There are things going on here that I don't understand."

As he spoke, the castle gates swung open, and a group of young elves rode into the courtyard on high-spirited black horses. The leader of the group waved a hand at Walter.

"Ho, Sir Knight! We're off to the hunting—will you come with us?"

Walter looked over at Randal, who shrugged. "Why not?" the young wizard said. "One kind of search is as good as another. Perhaps you'll find the High King's daughter on the way."

One of the elves brought forth a saddled horse. Walter mounted, and they rode off.

Lys and Randal continued onward. All at once, the sound of a clear voice singing came through an open door nearby, accompanied by the rippling notes of a harp.

"Music!" Lys cried out with a laugh, and she dashed away to seek its origin. The young wizard was left standing by himself in the courtyard.

The pleasures of Elfland have taken them both away, he thought. *Am I the only one who sees the cracks in the glass and the tarnish in the silver? The perfection that the others see can't be an illusion, or I would feel it at work— but what I'm seeing isn't an illusion either. Perhaps it's a different kind of reality, one meant for me alone.*

But why me? Randal couldn't think of an answer. He sighed. *I have to get away from here, so I can think.* He went out through the great gate of the castle, between pillars make of crystal inlaid with silver.

Outside the castle, he walked on to where a small hill, round and knoblike, rose above the smooth ground. *There was a hill like this not far from Castle Doun,* he remembered. *I used to climb it whenever I wanted to be really alone.*

What had been a good idea in those days seemed like an even better idea now. Randal climbed the hill and threw himself down on the springy turf to lie looking backward at the Erlking's castle. From this distance, the crystal towers glittered in the morning sunlight, and the traces of decay were invisible.

Lying there, Randal felt a sadness come over him. *So this is the Fair Realm that Master Madoc spoke of so longingly,* he thought. *It's not what I expected.*

He pushed himself back up to a sitting position and turned his back on the castle to look in the other direction. In the distance, he saw horsemen approaching—they rode black steeds, with green banners snapping in the wind. Randal felt a chill run down his back.

I've seen them before. The first day Master Madoc came to Castle Doun and read the future for us, I looked into the scrying-bowl, and I saw them. Then I saw them again in a dream, and that time they nearly caught me.

The horsemen rode like the wind with the

tattered banners flying above them. Randal wondered if he should run—but to where? Already, as he hesitated, the riders came nearer. He could see their pale faces beneath dark caps pinned with pheasant and eagle feathers or sprigs of flowering heather. Black cloaks streamed out behind them.

If I run, wondered Randal, *will I find myself trapped by invisible walls, the way I was in my dream?*

Then he shook his head. *That dream was a good one, in spite of all my fears—without it, I might never have chosen to follow the road to wizardry. I won't deny its power now by running away.*

Randal stood and faced the horsemen. They were close now, closer than they had ever come in that long-ago dream. He could see the teeth of the steeds, the horses' sides glistening with sweat and flecked with white foam. Straight up the hill swept the riders, charging toward Randal as he stood waiting.

The foremost rider leaned down from the saddle and extended an arm. Without slowing in his mad gallop, he caught Randal and swung the young wizard up onto the saddle behind him. Randal held tightly onto the rider's belt. *If I fall,* he thought, *I'll be trampled.* No one spoke; there was no sound except the thunder of hooves over that flawless grass and the snapping of the banners overhead.

The sky above them grew black with an approaching storm. The horsemen rode on, flying faster than the wind, leaving the grass behind and galloping over a broken jumble of rocks. They pulled up at last on the top of a low, bare hill, inside a circle of standing stones. A mighty chair carved from black rock stood in the midst of the tall stones, and on it sat a single elf garbed in robes like the night, with a silver circlet binding the black hair back from his forehead.

His face was pale and stern, with fathomless dark eyes shaded by black, level brows. Like the elf-maid and the elfin riders, he had a perfect symmetry about his features that was something more than human, and his entire bearing had a more than human majesty. This, Randal knew, could be none other than the king of all Elfland, the Erlking himself.

The elfin knights dismounted, and so did Randal. Thunder cracked and boomed overhead. Randal took a step forward toward the throne of the King of the Elves. The knights formed a semicircle behind him. Randal went down on one knee.

"You summoned me, Your Majesty."

"Yes." The Erlking's voice was deep and resonant, his gaze as dark as the storm clouds and as piercing as the lightning that laced the sky above. He looked at the young wizard for a long while without speaking further. It was all Randal could do to meet that unwavering regard without flinching.

"You know who I am," the Erlking said.

"Yes, Your Majesty. I know."

"But you know nothing of my nature." The Erlking stood and began to pace, his dark robes swirling about him like storm-tossed clouds. "You are a wizard in mortal lands, and so you know something of the laws binding magic. You cannot speak an untruth and expect magic to serve you truly thereafter. Here magic is purer, and far more strict a master. A mortal wizard can sometimes break the words of a promise in order to keep its spirit, but I cannot. If I say that I will do a thing, or that I will not do a thing—then I must do it, or leave it undone, exactly as the words were spoken."

He stopped in his pacing and sat down again upon his throne. Once more he fixed Randal with his dark, unblinking gaze. "So, young Randal— would you trade your mortal magic for the power of the Fair Realm, now that you know its price?"

Randal thought of all the times he had used half-truths to mislead others and ease his own way, and shook his head. "No, Your Majesty," he replied honestly.

Still kneeling, he looked up at the Erlking. "But I think your riders brought me here for something more than just the talk of magic. What is it you need from me that only a mortal wizard can provide?"

Thunder rumbled in the distance. "Save my kingdom," the Erlking said.

Randal thought of the grime and decay that only he seemed able to perceive. "How can I do that?"

But there was no answer, and Randal lowered his

eyes. He saw that the bare dirt beneath his feet had become lush green grass. The wild wind and the lightning were gone. Instead, a soft breeze blew through his hair, and sunlight warmed his neck.

He looked up again. The Erlking and all his knights had vanished. Now Randal knelt in a rose arbor, where large red and white blossoms covered the thorned greenery. The scent of the roses came to him on the breeze, but once again, under its sweetness, he caught the faint odor of decay.

Beneath the arbor, a young woman in a green silk dress sat alone on a bench of white marble. She seemed only a little older than Randal—his cousin Walter's age, perhaps—but the hair that flowed unbound to below her waist was the color of old silver. A banner of blue silk lay spread out across her lap. The needle in her hand carried a fine silver thread in and out of the fabric as she sat and sewed, working the images of a leaping deer and a kingly crown.

I've never seen that banner before, Randal thought, still kneeling. *But when I was a boy at Castle Doun, I used to hear Sir Iohan talk about how it flew over the Field of Kings on the day the High King was crowned. Those are the royal arms of Brecelande—and this must be the High King's daughter.*

He lifted his head. "My lady," he said, "I believe I know who you are. But your name is still a mystery to me."

The young woman looked at him, unsmiling. Her eyes, which were even greener than her dress, watched him with a steadiness almost as unsettling as the Erlking's darker regard. "I am Diamante," she said at last. "The King of Elfland's foster-daughter and blood daughter to the High King of Brecelande. You are . . . ?"

"Randal of Doun," he said. "A journeyman wizard and a friend to Master Madoc the Wayfarer, who brought you here." He paused, drew an unsteady breath, and went on. "Your true kingdom needs you, and I've come to bring you home."

The young woman took another stitch in the blue silk of the banner. "Years ago," she said, as her slender fingers pulled the silver thread through the cloth, "my foster-father gave his word to keep me here—and however greatly he may desire to send me back, or I may desire to go, the laws of Elfland will force him to keep the letter of his oath."

Randal thought about that for a moment. "Why would the Erlking want to send you home in the first place?" he said. "If he truly loves you as a daughter, he must know how dangerous such a journey would be."

"That may be so," Diamante said. "But as much as my foster-father cares for me, he cares for his kingdom more. Of all the places in the mortal world, the nearest to the Erlking's realm is Brecelande—the barriers between the worlds are thinnest there, and discord in my true kingdom brings decay to my adopted home. Surely you have seen it."

"I have," Randal admitted slowly, "but why is it that neither of my friends can see the cracks and the tarnish?"

"You are a wizard," said Diamante, "and have been trained to use your inward vision. You see the actual substance of a thing and not just the appearance that it happens to have in the world." The princess threaded another stitch through the silk of the banner. "But do not think ill of your friends—in this matter most of the elf-folk are as blind as they."

"The Erlking asked a mortal wizard to save his kingdom," murmured Randal. "But why me? I'm not even a master, only a journeyman."

"But you are the one who answered the call when it was given," said Diamante. "Tell me truthfully, Randal of Doun: You've dreamed of Elfland before now, have you not?"

"I didn't know then what I dreamed of," he said, recalling that long-ago nightmare. "But I did dream."

"Your dreams were my doing," she told him. "Messages sent out blindly, like boats of leaves and bark set afloat on a stream. I was searching for someone willing to free me; but the Erlking . . . who knows what he is searching for? Here in the Fair Realm his power is great, but he cannot act outside it."

A distant horn blew before Randal could speak. Diamante pulled her needle through the blue silk one more time, knotted the thread, and broke it off. "There, it is finished," she said. She folded the banner neatly and rose to her feet.

"We will speak more later, but now is not the time to make plans—the horn is the signal for the feasting. All the elfin court must attend, and you also, on pain of the Erlking's displeasure. Come with me."

She turned, still carrying the folded banner, and appeared to walk straight into the thorny green wall of the rose arbor. Randal stood and followed her. At the last moment, the leaves parted to reveal the great hall of the castle of gold and crystal. Not since his days at Prince Vespian's palace in Peda had Randal seen such splendor: beeswax tapers in gem-encrusted holders, tall mirrors reflecting the flickering points of light along the walls, and gold and silver everywhere.

The Erlking in his dark robes sat at the high table in the central chair. Diamante walked in and took a seat at the Erlking's left hand. She nodded at Randal to take a seat beside her. To the Erlking's right hand sat Sir Walter, and then Lys. "Our guests are here," the Erlking said. "Let the feast begin."

At his word, unseen musicians began to play. The soft melodies had an eerie beauty, reminding Randal of the illusory notes that Master Madoc had once called out of the air to entertain feasters at Castle Doun. *Was Madoc playing music that he heard during his own visit to Elfland?* Randal wondered. *Was that why the songs all sounded so sad?*

The phantom instruments played on. Platters of

food floated into the hall, as if carried in the hands of invisible servants, but without the resonance of magical power that would betray a levitation-spell in use. Dishes of silver and gold already lay at each place, and now hands that Randal couldn't see heaped the plates high with roasted meat and white bread.

Randal picked up the ivory-handled knife that lay beside his plate and cut off a bite-sized piece of meat. He hesitated a moment, the meat almost at his lips.

You've already tasted the fruits of Elfland, he thought. *Why hold back now?*

He bit into the chunk of meat. Only his childhood lessons in courtesy and his wizardly training in self-control kept him from crying out in disgust. The meat was too far gone in decay for even spices to disguise, and it was scorched besides.

He looked over at Lys and Walter, but the lute-player and the knight didn't seem to have noticed the foul taste. Neither did Diamante, closer by, although the steady coolness of her green eyes might have concealed almost any reaction. As for the Erlking—*Who knows what the King of the Elves thinks about anything?* Randal said to himself.

Randal forced himself to keep on eating. As he worked his jaws to chew and swallow the rotten meat, he looked about him and saw that here in the feast-hall, as earlier in the guest chambers, the splendor of Elfland seemed to have fallen into disrepair. The gold and silver plates were dented

27

and tarnished, and the crystal goblets beside them had chips knocked out of the rims.

The elfin music ended, and all the feasters applauded. Then the Erlking spoke to Lys.

"Sing for us, child, I pray you—for we of Elfland have a love of earthly music, and of all mortals, bards are the most dear to us."

Lys stood and bowed to the Erlking. "Gladly, Your Majesty. But my lute isn't here with me—do I have your leave to fetch it?"

"There's no need," said the Erlking. "Use this one."

He clapped his hands together once, and the same unseen servants that had brought the meat now carried forth a lute and presented it to Lys. The singer looked startled, but she slipped the lute's carrying-strap over her head and came out from behind the high table to stand before the Erlking and his foster-daughter. She paused for a moment, her expression thoughtful, while her hands roamed lightly over the strings of the lute. Then she began her song.

"Strange news is come to town,
Strange news is carried.
Some say my love is dead,
Some say he's married . . ."

Randal sat listening, as he had so many times before. As Lys sang, the world about him seemed to slow and then grow still, until he sat at the heart of a circle of calm.

Only once before had he known such a stillness, on a stormy night in Widsegard, when he had stood outside of time and spoken with the ghost of his teacher, Master Laerg. That night he had been near death himself, and stepping out of time had been perilously easy. Now he sat at a feast in Elfland, and he realized that the timelessness around him was the true nature of the Erlking's realm.

Then he saw that he was not alone in the circle of quiet. The Erlking had left the seat of honor and had come to stand at his shoulder. The young wizard turned and met the dark gaze of the King of the Elves.

"What do you want of me?" Randal asked.

"Talk," said the Erlking. "No more than talk. Does the feasting please you?"

Randal was silent. *A wizard doesn't lie. But a wise man doesn't anger a monarch in his own hall.*

"Come, come," said the Erlking. "What do you think of the food that we of Elfland eat?"

Randal drew a deep breath, and let it out slowly. *If he insists on dragging the truth from me,* he thought, *then let him have it without any sweetening.*

"They fed me better in Brecelande when I was a stableboy working for scraps from the table."

He expected an explosion of wrath, but none came. The Erlking only nodded and said, "So. And my feast-hall?"

"The silver is tarnished," said Randal. "And the glass is cracked."

"So," said the Erlking again. "One thing more,

young wizard—how stands the state of my kingdom?"

"In sore distress," said Randal. "Your fires give no heat, and the flowers are rotting even as they bloom."

Once again, the Erlking nodded. "Not many mortals can see the true nature of this place," he said to Randal. "You are one of the few. And not even my own people have the eyes to see the realm's decay. Only I see it, I and perhaps my mortal fosterling. . . . She has tried to escape back to her own realm half a dozen times, but the laws of this place have prevented her going. Now you see it also, and I know that you have come in answer to our need."

Randal opened his mouth to protest, but before the words came he felt the circle of quiet breaking. Once again, the Erlking sat in his chair, and Lys's song was drawing to an end.

"And as I thought on this,
I fell to weeping.
They stole my love away
While I was sleeping."

The elfin listeners cheered and applauded—and none louder than the Erlking himself.

"A performance fit for royalty in any land," he declared. "Only name your reward, my child, and you shall have it."

There was silence in the feast-hall. Lys glanced

over toward Randal, her blue eyes asking a silent question. Randal looked at the singer, and then at the Erlking. The Erlking said nothing. Randal turned back to Lys and nodded.

Lys gave him a quick smile and then turned to face the Erlking. When she spoke, her voice carried to the farthest corners of the hall.

"Give us your mortal foster-daughter, the true queen of Brecelande."

III.

Between the Worlds

IN AN INSTANT, all was dark, and the elfin feast-hall vanished. Instead, Randal stood in the midst of an empty plain. It was night, but off on the horizon, red-orange jets of fire lanced toward the sky, lighting the underbellies of heavy, low-hanging clouds.

He looked about and saw Walter, Lys, and the princess Diamante standing nearby. Diamante appeared unsurprised—and even, Randal thought, pleased—by the sudden turn of events. In her hands she still held the folded banner that she had carried with her from the rose arbor. Lys clutched her lute, and Walter had his sword out, ready for trouble.

The knight looked over at his cousin. "What did you just do, Randy?"

"He didn't do anything," said Lys. "The Erlking told me to name my own reward, and it seemed like too good a chance to pass up—but I don't think he's happy with us."

Diamante gave a soft laugh. "If my foster-father were angry," she said, "we wouldn't be here to talk about it."

"That's good to know," said Walter. "But not very helpful."

Randal shook his head. "I'm sure the Erlking put us here for his own reasons—but we don't have the time to waste in talking. The sooner we're out of here, the better."

"Well, then," said Walter, sheathing his sword, "which way do we go?"

Randal looked over at Diamante. The Erlking's foster-daughter pointed toward the horizon, where plumes of fire spouted heavenward. "That way."

The four companions started toward the flames. It was slow going. They had to pick their way over uneven ground full of lumps of black stone that rolled and twisted under their feet or reared up in grotesque boulders. After what seemed an endless, footsore journey, they came to a place where cracks in the ground spewed forth a red-gold spray of fire.

The travelers paused. Ahead of them, a narrow stream bubbled over the broken stone like a tangled skein of white yarn. Then another pillar of frozen fire sprang up from the gaping earth. It lit up the whole scene with a ruddy glow. Suddenly, Randal drew a sharp breath.

On the other side of the stream, outlined against the orange glow, dark shapes moved restlessly— four black horses, which were saddled, bridled, and riderless. A mounted knight in a black surcoat and black armor waited directly in front of the stream, blocking the way to the horses on the other side. A helm of black metal hid his features, and orange light reflected off the gleaming lance in his right hand. Another lance was planted point-first in the earth beside him.

"Go back," he said. "You shall not pass by me."

Walter took a step forward. "We must pass by if this is the way to our own country."

"Walter," said Randal quietly. "Be careful."

Walter looked over his shoulder at his cousin. "I know what I'm doing, Randy. This challenge is mine." He turned back to face the black knight. "Tell me truly—is this the road that leads to the mortal realm?"

"It is," said the knight. "But you cannot pass unless you fight me first."

"Then we fight," said Walter. "Let the prize be passage for myself and my friends."

"So be it," said the black knight. He raised a hand, and one of the four horses trotted forward, splashing through the stream to halt in front of Walter. A helmet and shield hung from the saddle, and Randal saw that the shield bore Walter's arms—a pine tree on a red and gold background.

Walter swung himself up into the saddle. He put the helm on his head and slipped his arm through the straps of the pine-tree shield. The black knight handed his own lance to Walter, then plucked the second lance out of the earth.

The two knights separated and rode until they stood about a hundred yards apart. Then they turned. The black knight clashed his lance against his shield by way of salute and rode at Walter. Walter clashed his own lance in answer and spurred forward into a gallop, shield before him and lance held high.

Clods of dirt flew upward from the horses' hooves as the two riders charged furiously at one another. They met with a crash—the noise of wood and steel and leather all crying out together under the impact. Walter's lance struck the center of his adversary's shield and splintered as it hit.

The force of the collision pushed the black knight backward in his saddle, but he kept his seat. His own lance slid off the edge of the pine-tree shield and caught Walter in the side. The sharpened metal point ripped apart the links of chain mail and opened a six-inch gash in the flesh over Walter's ribs.

At the sight of the wound, Randal clenched his fists and bit back a cry of dismay. *Whatever happens,* he ordered himself, *keep silent. Walter can't afford to be distracted from what he's doing.*

Both of the knights threw away their lances, drew their swords, and rode back toward one another. When they came together, Randal's cousin hooked his shield behind the black knight's and pulled, lifting his adversary up and forward out of the saddle.

The black knight fell headlong to the ground,

rolling to his feet as Walter dismounted. The two men came at one another, swords in hand, to continue the fight on foot. Randal saw the blood running down his cousin's armor from the gash in his side and watched fearfully as the two men circled one another.

Walter's good, he thought, *but he'll be weakening soon. He needs to end this in a hurry.*

The two knights fought on, churning the dirt to mud beneath their feet. Then, as Walter swung his sword to deliver another blow, he lost his footing on the slick mud and tumbled to the earth. The black knight didn't wait for Walter to rise, but drew the dagger from his belt and fell on top of him. As if in a nightmare, Randal watched the narrow blade come down, a metal snake seeking a weakness in Walter's armor.

Somehow, the blade struck the mail slantwise; it slid off without penetrating. Walter dropped his sword and grabbed the black knight by the shoulder. He threw a leg over the black knight's body and rolled his adversary under him.

Now Walter knelt, straddling the other knight. His left hand pinned down the wrist that held the dagger. Walter's own dagger was out; it was poised at the black knight's throat.

Walter spoke, his voice breathless and muffled by the closed helm. "Yield, Sir Knight, so my friends and I may pass."

"I yield," said the black knight. "You may go."

Walter rose and helped his former opponent to

his feet. The black knight pulled off his helm. Diamante cried out, and Randal stared—the black knight was none other than the Erlking himself.

"You've bested me in a fair fight," said the King of the Elves to Randal's cousin, "and have won ransom from me, as well as passage. Only name what I must pay."

This is the second time he's given one of us free choice, thought Randal. *Whatever ransom Walter asks, the Erlking will have to pay it—and no one who's bound so strictly to his given word is likely to make such an offer without thinking. There must be something he wants us to ask for, something that he can't give us otherwise. . . .*

But Walter already seemed to know the answer. "Your Majesty, only you know best what you are worth. Name your own ransom."

The Erlking smiled. "That was well chosen," he said. "The ransom is this: I will come to your aid when you call, wherever you may be. But you may make this request only once." Then he whistled for his black horse, climbed into the saddle, and rode away.

Walter sheathed his dagger. He then retrieved his sword and slid it back into the scabbard, and swung up into the saddle of his own horse. As he did so, the other three steeds trotted forward across the stream and stopped in front of Randal, Lys, and Diamante.

"Let's mount up and go," said Walter to Randal. "Elfland may be full of wonders, but I don't think it's a place where mortals ought to linger."

37

They crossed the stream and came out of the shallow water onto a morning-lit road, with a brook behind them and the same road continuing on its other side.

So easy a passage, Randal thought, *and so quick. Not like the shoreless sea we crossed to enter Elfland.*

The elfin steed beneath him moved restlessly as he looked about. A warm sun shone in the sky, and the road before them was well-tended. A few small green hills rose up on the horizon ahead. There was no sign of the barren, fire-blasted landscape where Walter had fought with the Erlking.

"Where are we now?" asked Diamante. "This is no place I have ever seen."

"We're in Brecelande," said Randal. "I know the feel of my own homeland well enough. But what part of the kingdom we've come to, I can't say."

Walter was frowning. "We have more problems than that, Randy. Smell the air, and look at the wildflowers by the road—it's springtime here, and it was autumn when we left the northern borders. Those few hours we spent in Elfland turned into six months while we were gone."

"And you're still wounded," said Lys. "We'll have to stop soon and let Randy take care of you."

"We may not have time," said Diamante, her voice tight but controlled. "Look behind us."

Randal turned in his saddle and saw close to two dozen mounted men coming into view on the road beyond the stream. At the sight of Randal and his companions, the riders proceeded faster, increasing their speed from a walk to a canter, and then to a trot.

"Too many to stand and fight," Randal said. "I'll throw a spell of confusion onto the road behind us—that should have them going in circles from now until midnight, at least."

He wheeled his horse to face the oncoming riders and chanted the words that would put a web of illusions and false trails between himself and them. He felt the power of the spell go forth, then sensed it fade without taking effect.

They're enchanted against the power of magic, he thought, *which means they came expecting to deal with a wizard—and that means a wizard must have sent them.*

"It's no good," he called to Walter, trying to keep the sudden fear out of his voice. "We'll have to run."

They rode, and the strangers behind them followed steadily. Randal began to wonder why their pursuers didn't put on any more speed—and then another two dozen mounted men came around the nearest hill and galloped out onto the road ahead.

"Now we *are* trapped," said Walter, drawing his sword. "There's nothing for it but to fight."

"Not yet," said Diamante. "Follow me."

She turned her horse off the road and headed straight for the grass-covered slope of the hill in front of them. Just as the rose arbor had parted for her in the Erlking's realm, so did the side of the green hill; Randal, Lys, and Walter rode behind the princess into an echoing, underground place.

"Where are we?" Randal asked, looking about at the heavy cut stone that roofed the bare, open chamber like a dome under the earth. Doorways shaped like gaping mouths opened off the central room. The horses stamped and nickered in a reddish light that seemed to come from everywhere and nowhere at once.

"We're in an elfin fort," Diamante answered. "My foster-father's people have them scattered over this world, as places of rest and refuge for travelers."

"Why haven't we seen them before?" he asked.

"Because before this you had never eaten the fruit of Elfland," she said. "I can see them because I was fostered among the elves, and now you'll be able to find them as well."

"About time you got here," said a rough voice from one of the doorways. "I've been waiting since His Majesty sent me word that you'd be coming. But who are these with you?"

The speaker, a tall elf with reddish-brown hair and a short, bushy beard, came forward, bowed his head briefly to the princess, and then took the horses' bridles.

"It's good to see you, Ullin," said Diamante as she and the others dismounted. She indicated her three companions. "These are Randal, Walter, and Lys. They are the ones who answered my call."

"I'd hoped for more than three humans to help you," said Ullin. "Because if you aren't crowned High Queen of Brecelande on Midsummer's Day, it will be the worse for both kingdoms."

"How long does that give us?" Walter asked. "And what part of Brecelande is this?"

"This is the Barony of Wirrell," Ullin replied, "close by the Wilderness of Llannad. And as for time—you have two months, and you'll need every minute." He looked the three of them up and down. "If you're the ones who can do it."

Under the gaze of the red-haired elf, Randal felt compelled to speak. "I went to Elfland to rescue the princess and to restore her kingdom if it is possible to do so. I have not changed my purpose."

Walter's back straightened. "Nor have I," the knight said to Ullin. "I will see the princess Diamante safely on her throne or perish myself in the attempt."

Lys's face was pale, but her voice was firm as she added, "Brecelande isn't my country, but I'm not deserting my friends as long as they may need my help."

Ullin nodded. "Your summoning worked well," he said to Diamante. "These three may yet serve your need."

To Randal, Ullin seemed at once respectful and commanding. *If a man could be both a peasant and a king in the same moment*, Randal thought, *I suppose he would behave much the same.*

The tall elf led the horses away down the side tunnel, and Randal joined Lys and Diamante near the opening of the elf-fort. The archway through which they had entered seemed like a green veil over the road and the pleasant valley. Behind them,

41

Walter prowled about the boundaries of the central chamber with his sword in his hand.

"This place did not always belong to the elves," Walter said, "and it has a strange feel to it. What was it before?"

"Like the other elfin forts, it was once a grave of men," Diamante replied. "But through the centuries, the Erlking's folk took them over and fashioned them into havens for the needy."

Lys moved her feet uneasily and glanced back over her shoulder at the round chamber. "A grave," the lute-player said to Randal. "And that green haze between us and the road is the earth we're looking through. Did we die in that place you call Elfland, and are we dead and buried now?"

It was Diamante who answered. "This much is true: You died to the old way of looking at the world around you. Before, you saw only a part of it. Now, you see more."

"I'm not sure I like that," said Walter. "I already saw everything I needed to and never asked for anything else."

His voice had a sharp note in it that wasn't like his usual, cheerful tone. Randal turned and saw that his cousin looked pale, even in the reddish light. A dark splotch stained his left side where the Erlking's lance had ripped through his mail coat and torn the flesh beneath.

"Are you still bleeding?" Randal demanded. "Take off your armor and let me do something about it."

In the end, Randal had to help his cousin remove the heavy chain mail and the bulky quilted arming-coat underneath it. A sluggish trickle of blood ran down from the long gash in the knight's flesh. Randal convinced Walter to lie down with the arming-coat for a pillow, and then worked the spells to stop the bleeding and close the wound.

When the healing was done, Walter slept next to the wall of the underground chamber. While he rested, Randal and Lys shared the food that Ullin brought them, and night fell outside the elf-mound. It was dark outside before Walter awoke and joined the others.

"Thank you," he said to Randal. "That wound wouldn't have killed me outright, but it would have slowed me down for weeks. I can't afford that right now." The knight turned to Diamante. "Why did the Erlking challenge me after he'd let us go?"

"No one wins free of the Fair Realm easily," said the princess. "Especially not when its ruler has sworn an oath that one of those leaving shall stay. By his word to Lys, he had to send me forth . . . but his earlier vow still bound him."

"So it did, Your Highness," said Ullin. The red-haired elf came out of the inner recesses of the grave-mound and began clearing away the scraps of food. "And more than that—he cares for you as he would a true daughter. Do you think that he'd let you go in the company of anyone he didn't know was worthy of the trust?"

A test, thought Randal. *The single combat was a test.*

But there's more to it than that, I think . . . or why would he have offered Walter a ransom when all they fought for was passage?

Walter was nodding gravely at Ullin's words. "The Erlking was right to expect trouble," he said. "It's six months or more since we left Brecelande, but somebody is already chasing us."

"I want to know how they found us," said Lys. "We didn't even know ourselves where we were going to show up."

"I don't know who's on our trail," Randal said, "but he's got a master wizard working for him— one skilled enough to work a scrying-spell that would tell him exactly where to look for us, and powerful enough to protect all those men-at-arms against magical attack at the same time."

"Somebody doesn't want to see me crowned as queen," said Diamante. She looked at Randal and the others. "I know I must present myself to the earls on the Field of Kings on Midsummer's Day. I will do this despite any lord or wizard who wishes to stand in my way. But you three know this land, and I don't. If you have advice, I will hear it."

"We should go to Castle Doun," said Randal, without hesitation. "Lord Alyen will shelter us for our own sakes, while we plan what to do next."

"Father can help you with that part," said Walter. "Ask him in my name—"

"What do you mean, 'in your name'?" Randal stared at his cousin with sudden concern. "You're not—"

Walter laughed. "Don't worry, Randy. You've done a good job of patching me together. But I think that I ought to ride out on my own tomorrow, while you three go to Castle Doun."

"What for?" asked Lys.

"No matter how good the princess's claim may be," said Walter, "the sad fact is that nothing gets done in Brecelande these days without an army. So I'm going to go look for one."

Randal shook his head. "Even in Brecelande, armies don't just lie on the ground like windfall apples."

"No, they don't," agreed Walter. "But while I'm not the friend of any great lord, I do happen to know one, and he is master of these lands hereabout. I'm going to pass the word to him and to the knights who ride from tourney to tourney that the High Queen has returned. I have something of a reputation in these parts—I never asked for one, but I seem to have it just the same—and if I raise up the true queen's banner, I think that there are those who will follow it."

IV.
Castle Doun

THEY SPENT THE night in the chamber beneath the ground. Randal expected to have bad dreams, but he slept deeply and well. In the morning, when the first bright sunlight shone in through the veil of earth, Ullin brought out the four black horses from the depth of the elf-fort.

Walter was the first to mount. "I'm off," he said to Randal as he swung into the saddle. "Give Father my respects, and tell him we'll meet at midsummer, if not before."

He rode out through the door of the elf-fort, and soon all that Randal could see of him was the sunlight glinting off his armor.

The young wizard turned to Ullin. "You've watched the comings and goings of men. Can you tell us the shortest way to Castle Doun?"

"If you want the shortest way," said the red-haired elf, "I can show you the road. If you want the fastest way, and the safest, then you'll have to come with me on the straight track between the elf-forts—but that's not a journey most mortals would care to make."

"We'll follow your lead," said Randal. "Someone's already tried to stop us once, and I won't feel safe until we've got castle walls around us."

"Then ride out," said Ullin, "and let the horses shadow my footsteps."

The elf strode out the door of the grave-mound, and Randal and the others rode after him. Turning back, Randal saw that the fort once again appeared as a low, round hill. If he looked closely, he could see the outline of the entrance in its side, like a deeper green shadow on the dense grass.

Ullin ignored the roadway that formed a brown stripe across the landscape and struck out instead in a straight line toward the south. At first he set an easy, steady pace, but as he walked he began to go faster and faster, without ever seeming to lengthen his stride. Soon, the horses had to trot to keep up with him.

The red-haired elf continued to quicken his pace as they went, until they traveled at a headlong gallop—but still he rode on ahead of them. The sky above turned black as they rode, and the wind grew loud. The lakes and streams along their route were whipped into a white foam, and green leaves stripped from branches swirled in a dense cloud around them. The horses plunged and reared.

They rode on, while lightning flashed in white sheets overhead and thunder boomed like a steady roll of drums. The earth churned to mud under the horses' hooves, and cold water ran like a river in their way. But still they galloped southward, always in a straight line, as the wind howled and flocks of dark-winged birds flew cawing around them. At last, they rode into the open side of another elf-fort.

"We're here," said Ullin. "Beyond this fort, there's nothing but men."

The wind died down as he spoke. The clouds parted, and Randal saw through the opening in the side of the elf-fort the familiar shape of Castle Doun.

At the sight of the weathered gray walls, Randal urged his horse forward out of the elf-mound—the same low green hill that had been his childhood refuge and that had held him trapped in his dream of wizardry. Lys and Diamante followed, but Ullin shook his head.

"I'll stay here where it's safe," he said.

Randal was already halfway down the slope toward Castle Doun. *I knew I missed this place,* he thought, *but I never realized how much I longed for it until I saw it again.*

He slowed his pace as he drew nearer. He'd expected things to change at his uncle's castle during the years he'd been gone—but what he was seeing now wasn't just a difference made by the passage of time. Around the castle, the fields where the peasants worked to raise the crops were bare and untended, and the cottages of Doun village stood empty. Everything was silent. No plowmen called to their teams of oxen, no ring of hammer on anvil sounded from the blacksmith's workshop, no voices rose in scolding or laughter.

Lys rode up beside him. "What's wrong?"

He bit his lip. "I don't know. But something . . . look at the castle. The gates are closed. That never used to happen in the daytime. And look there." He pointed at the castle's highest watchtower, where a red and gold banner waved on the morning wind.

"That's Lord Alyen's own banner—the big one. It's only flown for important reasons."

There was a moment of silence from Lys before she asked, "What kind of important reasons?"

"I only saw it once," Randal said, "for a wedding in the family." Then another possibility came to him like a cold hand gripping his insides. He urged his elfin steed to a gallop, riding straight for the castle gates.

He was barely within hailing distance when a voice shouted from the walls, "Who goes there?"

"Randal, nephew to Lord Alyen," he shouted back.

"Who rides with you?"

Randal looked over his shoulder at Lys and Diamante, coming up behind him at a slower pace. *If I can't give the High King's daughter her true name here, of all places, then there's no hope for us at all.*

"Demoiselle Lys of Occitania," he shouted back at the watchman, "and the princess Diamante, true heir to Brecelande."

There was a pause, and then the watchman

49

shouted down, "Come forward and be recognized."

Randal and his two companions rode on up to the small entrance—no wider and higher than would admit one man at a time on foot—that still stood open next to the main gate. Randal dismounted and went forward alone, leading his horse.

"Here I am," he said to the guard. "Is Sir Palamon or Sir Iohan here? They would know me."

"No need," said the guard. "Pass on through— Lord Alyen has been expecting you."

For a moment, Randal felt almost weak-kneed with relief. *Whatever's wrong, at least Lord Alyen is still well.* Then confusion began to creep in. *But . . . expecting me? How can that be, when I've been gone from the world for six months, and yesterday morning I didn't even know where I was?* He suppressed the urge to pelt the guard with questions and gestured to Lys and Diamante to dismount and follow him.

Once through the narrow passage from the side gate to the courtyard, Randal paused again. In contrast with the deserted village outside the walls, the main courtyard of Castle Doun was choked with a milling crowd of people and animals. There were so many that the dust raised by their feet filled the air with a golden haze.

What's going on here? Randal wondered. *It looks like the castle's preparing for a siege, but there's no army camped outside the walls.*

At a shout from the guard, a man in chain armor strode toward Randal, Lys, and Diamante. He wore a surcoat in Doun's colors of red and gold, and a broadsword swung at his hip.

"Sir Palamon," Randal whispered. Doun's master-at-arms had been his first teacher, long before he'd dreamed of leaving the barony to study magic. There'd been a time when Palamon's opinion of him had mattered more to Randal than anything else in the world . . . *but I remember him as taller, somehow,* Randal thought.

The master-at-arms came to a halt a yard from where Randal stood. He looked Randal up and down, once, with an appraising glance. Then he stepped forward and crushed the young wizard in a tremendous bear hug.

"Randal!" he exclaimed. "I'd given up hope of seeing you again. But you've come back, and in high time, too. I'm glad to see you—and your companions, as well."

Diamante stepped forward. "Where are the lord and lady of this castle? I must speak with them."

"This way, my lady," Sir Palamon replied. The knight led them through the crowded courtyard and up the stairs to the great hall. The long, high-ceilinged chamber was even noisier and more crowded than Randal remembered it. *Everyone in Doun who wasn't in the courtyard must be here,* he thought as the racket assaulted his ears.

"Randal!" cried another familiar voice. "It's good to have you back—I didn't think we'd ever see you again, in spite of what that wizard said."

The crowd parted, and his Aunt Elene, Walter's

51

mother, swooped down to enfold him in a warm embrace that smelled of dried lavender and new-spun wool. She was bubbling over with questions. "Are you well? Have you seen Walter? Is he well? And your friends—who are they?"

"I'm fine," he told Lady Elene. "The last time I saw Sir Walter was somewhere up in the north country. And my friends are Demoiselle Lys and the princess Diamante."

Lady Elene's eyes widened. " 'Princess' . . ." she murmured. Then she recovered her composure and said briskly, "Your uncle will want to talk with you about that, I'm sure. But all three of you look worn out from hard riding—let me see about getting you food and a place to rest."

Diamante shook her head. "We have to see Lord Alyen before all else."

Randal was surprised when Lady Elene didn't object—in the old days, no one would have dreamed of questioning her. *Of course, I didn't bring home princesses in the old days either,* he thought, as Lady Elene replied, "As you wish, my lady," to Diamante, then hurried off and left them alone with Sir Palamon.

The master-at-arms led them up the tower stairs to Lord Alyen's private chambers. At the door, Sir Palamon knocked and entered. Randal hung back, remembering his days as a squire in the castle, when he carried trays of meat to his uncle's table and spoke only when he was spoken to. Now there was Palamon—the idol and terror of his childhood—treating him like an honored guest. It made him uncomfortable.

The master-at-arms looked over his shoulder at Randal. "Come in, come in," he said.

Randal and his companions followed Sir Palamon into the chamber. Lord Alyen was sitting with Sir Iohan, the eldest of Castle Doun's household knights. A sheet of parchment lay on the table between them. A candlestick and a pewter goblet held down its curling ends. As Randal walked in with Lys and Diamante, both men rose to their feet.

Once again, Randal was struck by the changes time had wrought. Lord Alyen was still a tall, strongly built man with shoulders wide enough to carry all the burdens of Castle Doun, but now deep lines of worry marked his face. Sir Iohan's hair had just been turning gray at the temples when Randal left; now it was completely white.

Lord Alyen was the first to speak. "So you've come back, just as the wizard predicted. Is it true, then, what he told us was the reason for your return?"

"I don't know what he told you," Randal said. He drew a deep breath and continued. "I've come with the princess Diamante, the sole heir of the High King, and I ask your help to restore her to her throne."

Sir Iohan turned pale and sank back into his chair. "Then it is true," he whispered. "All my life I've hoped—but I never allowed myself to believe I

would see it happen. If only it isn't too late. . . ."

Randal was as unnerved as the old knight seemed to be. "Please, uncle," he said to Lord Alyen. "I've been on a long journey and have heard almost no news. What has happened in Brecelande these six months past—and why is Doun Castle making ready to stand a siege?"

"Can you read?" Lord Alyen said, by way of answer.

Randal nodded.

"Then take a look at this. Every baron and castellan in the realm received one." Lord Alyen picked up the square of parchment from the table and handed it to Randal.

The young wizard scanned the page quickly, from the text to the ribbons and flat seals of red wax that dangled from the lower edge. What he read explained Sir Iohan's fears and made Randal's own heart seem to stand still: The parchment bore a demand that Lord Alyen come forward and swear fealty or else forfeit his castle and lands. The proclamation bore the seal of Hugo de la Corre, High King of Brecelande.

Randal stood unmoving, the stiff sheet of parchment trembling in his hand. *So it's all no good. Somebody else has claimed the throne.*

"I received this last autumn," Lord Alyen was saying, "just before the first snow. Hugo de la Corre—do you believe it?"

"De la Corre," said Randal slowly. He was beginning to regain his mental balance, but the proclamation still wasn't making sense. "He doesn't have any claim to the throne. He isn't even one of the great lords."

Diamante held out her hand, and Randal passed the parchment over to her. She scanned it quickly, then handed the document back to Randal before turning to face Lord Alyen and Sir Iohan.

"What did you do about the swearing?" she asked.

Sir Iohan took up the tale. "We ignored his commands all winter. Then, a week ago, a herald came here wearing Hugo's colors and asked for our reply. We told him that we would give him our answer on Midsummer's Day."

Diamante looked at the two men. Though she wore no crown, she held her head as though Brecelande's royal circlet already rested on her silvery hair. "The time for waiting is past," she told them. "Give me your answer, here and now."

Lord Alyen regarded her for a long time in his turn. "We had already determined not to swear fealty, but to raise our own banner and make the castle ready for war," he said slowly. "Now that you have come into Brecelande with a wizard to uphold your claim and declare it to be valid, I offer my loyalty and obedience to you instead—and I offer my men, my castle, and my lands as well."

"I accept your fealty," the princess said simply. She took the bundle of blue cloth she'd carried with her ever since leaving the Fair Realm and unfolded it, spreading the expanse of silk out on the table before Lord Alyen and Sir Iohan. "I may not be able to keep the war away from your lands, but if it must come, at least you can fight beneath the banner of Brecelande."

"War," Randal said unhappily into the long silence that followed. He'd always cherished the memory of Castle Doun as a strong place untouched by the troubles that plagued the rest of Brecelande. "Doun won't stand alone against de la Corre, I hope."

"It's hard to tell," said Lord Alyen. "We haven't gotten much news lately, but what we hear is that half the lords of Brecelande are up in arms over his demands."

"But what about the remaining lords?" asked Diamante. "Will they support de la Corre?"

"Some will be silent out of fear," said Sir Iohan, looking grave. "But many of them honestly believe that any king is better than no king at all."

"Very well," said Diamante. "Send out messengers to those lords who have not sworn allegiance to de la Corre. Give them greetings, and call them in my name to meet me on the Field of Kings on Midsummer's Day."

Sir Palamon looked at Lord Alyen. Alyen nodded, and the master-at-arms left to carry out the princess's bidding.

"Better a war than Hugo de la Corre," said Lord Alyen when the knight had gone. "He's got nothing but his own strength to keep the earls loyal to him—the first man who thinks he's stronger than the king will snatch the crown for himself, and we'll see the whole blood-soaked business starting over again."

"How did everything happen so quickly?" Randal asked. "There wasn't any hint of this last summer."

"Last summer," said Lord Alyen, "no one could make a move unless Lord Fess or Duke Thibault backed him, and those two balanced each other. When both of them vanished at Bell Castle, and the last person who had any real claim to the crown vanished along with them—well, after that it was just a matter of time before some lord put himself on the throne. De la Corre was simply the one who acted first."

Randal looked down again at the parchment he held in his hands. *So I brought this trouble on Doun myself,* he thought, *when I broke the protective spells on Bell Castle and helped Lady Blanche run away from a kingdom she didn't want.*

"Surely Fortune is jesting with us," Sir Iohan said, "to bring us the true heir that we've needed for so long, now that it may be too late for her to gain her father's throne." The old knight heaved a deep sigh. "The last twenty years were bad enough, but I may yet be thankful that at my age I'm not likely to see the next twenty."

"I'll do what I can to make them good years for Brecelande, instead of bad," Randal promised. "But I wish we had another wizard here to help me handle this."

"We do have one," said Lord Alyen to Randal unexpectedly. "The wizard who warned us of your coming is still with us. But he hasn't come out of his tower room—not to eat, not to drink, not to speak with anyone—since the day he got here."

"I'd better see him," Randal said. "Maybe he needs help."

Or maybe he needs stopping, he added to himself. *No one has named this wizard yet—if Madoc had come here, I think Lord Alyen would have said so. And that ambush on the road yesterday is proof that I've got an enemy somewhere among the kingdom's wizards.*

"This is something Randal needs to do alone," he heard Lys saying in a soft voice to Princess Diamante as he left the chamber with Sir Iohan. "In the meantime, I think we should take up that offer of food and a place to rest."

While Lys and Diamante went downstairs to the hall, Sir Iohan led Randal up the stairs to one of the tower rooms—the same one that Madoc the Wayfarer had been given when he'd come to Castle Doun as a guest so long ago. Randal knocked on the door. When nobody answered, he gave it a gentle push. He felt a wizard's spell of locking fall away at his touch. The door opened, and he entered.

A familiar figure stood inside a magic circle glowing with mystic fire: not Madoc, but Master Crannach, one of the Regents of the Schola Sorceriae in Tarnsberg. The master wizard's usually elegant robes were stained, and sweat ran down his face. The glowing red letters around the border of his circle were written in blood, and blood stained the wide bandage around his hand.

Randal listened for several minutes to the spell that Crannach was chanting, then turned and shut the door behind him.

"What's going on?" Sir Iohan whispered.

"Powerful magic," said Randal. "Only the very strongest spells need to be sealed in blood. Master Crannach is doing his best to put up a barrier between this world and the demonic plane."

V.
High Table

SIR IOHAN uttered a startled oath, but Randal wasn't listening. He was already climbing the stairs to the solar—an airy, sunlit room where Lady Elene worked at spinning, weaving, and embroidery in happier times. His aunt would have taken Lys and Diamante there, away from the noise and crowds in the great hall. Right now he needed to talk with both of his companions, Diamante in particular.

He knocked on the door, and then went in. Lys and the princess sat together over a makeshift meal—bread, cheese, and a pitcher of the sparkling cider from the apples that grew in the orchards of Doun village. Lady Elene wasn't with them. Randal supposed that she'd gone back down to the great hall to try to create some order out of the chaos that was reigning there. Both Diamante and Lys looked up as he came in.

"You look like death warmed over," said Lys. "What else has gone wrong?"

"Everything," Randal said, as he sank wearily

into the room's only remaining chair. "Hugo de la Corre isn't the worst of it. Master Crannach from the Schola is here at Doun, and he's working powerful magic to put up barriers between this world and the demonic plane. From the feel of his spell-casting, I think he believes that the demons are close to breaking through."

"Demons?" asked Lys. "I thought we'd seen the last of them, after you helped Master Balpesh push the demon Eram back through the gate between the worlds."

Diamante paused, the silver knife in her hand poised above an uncut wedge of cheese. "I know too little of the ways of mortal wizards," she said. "I have only the elfin magic I learned in the Fair Realm, and such charms are ill-suited for combat. Is this Master Crannach strong enough to hold the demons back?"

"I hope so," said Randal. "At the Schola, he was the master who'd made a special study of demons and elementals and artifacts of power. If he can't do it, nobody can."

"Why don't you try a scrying-spell?" suggested Lys. "That way, you'll know at least what dangers to guard against."

"Maybe," said Randal. "Looking into the future is uncertain at best. If you don't ask the right questions, the answers you get can mislead you. But I'm willing to try."

He glanced about the solar. The tower chamber was crowded with embroidery frames and spindles and baskets of yarn, and the small loom his Aunt Elene used for fine weaving took up space at one side. "Give me something to focus on," he said. "A mirror, a crystal, a bit of polished metal."

Lys drank off the last cider remaining in her pewter goblet, then set the goblet in the center of the table and refilled it. "Will this do?"

"As well as anything else," said Randal.

He looked over at Diamante. The Erlking's foster-daughter sat leaning forward as if she, too, expected to see visions in the goblet. Her silvery hair hung down in front of her shoulders.

"What question shall we ask?" he inquired.

"Ask of my future in general," she said. "There may be more dangers than just demons to reckon with."

Randal cleared his mind and concentrated. Light and shadow moved across the surface of the liquid in the goblet. He strove to look past them into the depths. At last, a tiny spot of color appeared in the bottom of the cup. The color this time was brown, the color of dirt, or of dried blood.

I don't like the looks of this, Randal thought, but he kept on watching.

The spot of color spread to fill the whole cup. Then the picture opened up, and he could see that the dirt—or blood—covered a crown, lost and lying on a barren slope of tumbled, ashy rock. Above the slope, a bird of prey circled as if looking for a small animal to carry off.

The bird gave a cry and plummeted earthward.

It landed on the wrist of a man dressed in courtly finery, but with a warrior's sword hanging at his side in a battered scabbard. The lord was a strong man, heavyset, although not fat, and had straight red hair hanging to his shoulders.

He looked about him arrogantly and tossed the bird into the air again. It circled once, and then plunged onto the crown, lighting on it and crying out in a harsh voice.

But before the knight could reach the crown, another hand plucked it from the ground. The hand was lean and wrinkled; it was that of an old man clothed in the rich, symbol-embroidered robes of a master wizard. The bird vanished, and the wizard held the crown above his own head. The lord approached the wizard and grabbed the crown. Then both men stood on a grassy mound that rose up, somehow, within the gloomy hall of a castle.

The two men held the crown between them. As Randal watched, it grew smaller and smaller, shrinking away to nothing. Then the crown was gone, and the mound disappeared into the floor of the castle, shifting down like sand in the top part of an hourglass. At last, the castle collapsed and crumbled into ruins.

The two men stood unmoving all this time. As the mound dwindled away beneath them, they themselves began to change. They altered in shape and size until they no longer looked human at all, but more like unnatural creatures who had stolen the robes of lord and wizard. Randal looked closer, trying to make out their new features more clearly, but the picture remained dark and murky—then, without warning, the darkness was filled with a brilliant, painful burst of light.

Randal cried out and swept the goblet away from him. It fell over, spilling out its contents in a wave across the tabletop. Lys and Diamante gasped in alarm, but he ignored them; he sat hunched over with his face in his hands, waiting for the blaze and dazzle to fade from behind his eyelids.

He heard Lys and Diamante mopping up the spilled cider. Then Lys asked, "What's wrong, Randy? What did you see?"

The after-images were fading now. He took his hands away from his face and blinked to clear his vision. The two girls were both staring at him, their faces pale and fearful.

"I saw a lord and a wizard," Randal said finally. "I didn't recognize either one, but I'll bet the lord is this Hugo de la Corre who's calling himself High King these days. And the wizard—I don't know."

"You still haven't told us what went wrong," said Diamante.

He shook his head. "I'm not certain. But I *think* somebody detected my scrying and acted to stop it."

"The wizard?" Diamante asked.

"Maybe," said Randal. He frowned and shook his head to drive away the last floating dots of light. "If it was, I hope it was the same wizard who found us coming out of Elfland and set up that ambush.

Two enemies of such strength would be too much for a master to handle, let alone me."

"What do we do now?" asked Lys.

"Wait," said Randal. "Wait for Walter to get here, wait for de la Corre to make his next move, and wait for Master Crannach to finish his spells . . . but I don't think we'll have to wait for long."

That night at dinner, Randal sat at Lord Alyen's right hand. Lys and Diamante sat with Lady Elene at Alyen's left. Squires brought food to the tables. Randal didn't recognize them, although some of them were his own age, and some younger than he had been when he left. The meal was simple — plain roasted meat and boiled vegetables, with common brown bread even for the diners at the high table — and the portions were small.

Bad harvests, he thought, *even here. And Aunt Elene's being careful with the provisions.*

He turned to Lord Alyen. "Do you expect a siege?" he asked quietly, under the cover of conversation in the crowded hall. "Doun was never so important before that anyone had to take it."

Lord Alyen looked thoughtful. "No one ever tried to claim the throne before this," he said. "And there's no castle closer to the Field of Kings. If we're still holding out against the usurper by midsummer, we mock his crowning there and make a rallying point for those who oppose him."

"I see," said Randal. He left unspoken the thought that it wasn't long until midsummer, and that even in a year of bad harvests, Doun looked like too well-fed a barony to be starved quickly into surrender. If de la Corre truly wanted the castle, he would have to take it by storm—and that was no subject for the dinner table.

Randal tried to think of something else to talk about. As he thought, a wind blew in through the high, narrow windows of the hall, stirring up a spiral whirl of dust in the center of the floor. The air grew darker to Randal's sight, as if something invisible were sucking all the light from the torches.

The lean gray hunting dogs that ranged about the great hall howled at the change in the air, and then crept, whimpering, to lie at Lord Alyen's feet. But, to Randal's surprise, nobody except the dogs seemed to have noticed anything. The men and women at the high table continued to talk and eat and gaze about them just as if nothing was happening.

Randal looked over at Lys and Diamante. His companions were staring at the center of the room. *No, they see it, too,* he thought. *It's the fruits of Elfland, letting us see things most people can't.*

In the center of the room, the dust continued to swirl, rising to man-height and then higher. The dark cloud came together into a human shape, something with arms and legs and a head, but all distorted and misshapen. The creature moved forward on its thick, stubby legs, outlined in motes of dust that glittered in the torchlight, and started toward Diamante.

I have to do something, Randal thought. He pushed back the chair he sat on and stood.

"Randal?" came Lord Alyen's voice at his elbow. "Are you all right?"

Randal ignored him. The creature of dust and wind moved slowly but steadily, and every dragging step brought it nearer to where the princess sat. *I need to know what I'm dealing with,* thought the journeyman wizard, and he called out the words that would reveal a thing's true source and nature.

His spell showed a shadow of a wizard in the center of the hall—a lean, white-bearded man in a robe embroidered with mystic symbols. He stood in the middle of a glowing circle and spoke, but Randal heard no words.

It's the wizard from my vision, realized Randal. *He's at work in a circle somewhere, sending this thing against us—but why? And what do I do?*

Crannach would know. But Crannach isn't here.

Randal was vaguely aware of Lord Alyen pulling at the sleeve of his robe and Lady Elene making distressed noises farther down the high table. But they took up only the edges of his attention. All the rest was fixed on the dust-creature and its shambling progress toward Diamante's chair. The glittering dust motes that outlined the shuffling figure swirled about as it moved, as if stirred by the slow breeze of its passage.

A breeze, thought Randal. *Air. It's a creature made of dust and air. If air brought it into being, air can send it away. If only I can work fast enough—*

Heedless of his Aunt Elene's sharp outcry, he snatched the tall silver cup that stood by Lord Alyen's place and spilled out the wine in a crude circle on the tablecloth. With a finger dipped into the red liquid, he marked the four directions, the names of summoning, and the words of power. He grabbed four candles and their holders, and placed them around his hastily constructed circle.

I haven't got enough time to go through the whole spell—I'll have to get by on strength of will alone and hope it works.

He cried out those syllables of the Old Tongue that formed the bare bones of the spell, the few words that could not be omitted even in the direst need, and called up an air elemental.

The elemental appeared in the circle as a wavering figure, a tiny, man-shaped blur in the air.

"What is your name?" Randal asked it.

"Gyreleaf . . ." came the answer, like a whisper in his mind.

"Gyreleaf," Randal said, "I have a task for you." He pointed to the hulking dust-shape. "Do you see that creature of air?"

"I see it . . ."

"Break it up. Destroy it. Return it to the air it's made of. Then go."

"I shall . . ."

With a sweep of his hand across the tablecloth, Randal broke the circle. The air elemental sprang free and flashed toward the shape of dust like an almost visible streak of light. The looming figure

69

seemed to explode, losing its shape entirely as the sparkling motes of dust began to drift away like blowing streamers.

In the center of the hall, the shadow of the wizard in his phantom circle grew fainter. Finally, the creature of air was destroyed. The link broken, the image winked out.

The hall was full of light and sound again. Voices assaulted Randal's ears: Lys, exclaiming, "What *was* that thing, Randy; what did you do to it?"; his aunt, demanding to know if he were well; Sir Palamon, inquiring if he'd suddenly gone mad. Only his uncle seemed calm, despite the spilled wine and the ruined tablecloth—his uncle, and Diamante.

The princess rose from her seat and spoke to Randal directly. "I thank you for saving my life. I don't know who sent that thing, or for what it was intended—but I do know it meant to do me harm." Turning to Lord Alyen, she said, "I am tired. I'll be in my room if need arises." She left the hall. Lys went with her.

When they had gone, Randal sank back into his chair. He felt too exhausted to move. The effort of summoning the air elemental with only the barest hint of a spell had left him sweating. *If that was the wizard who scryed our appearance and set the ambush, he's traced us to Castle Doun, and we're all in danger.*

He sighed. *I'll have to do something to protect us—I wish I knew what would work. If only Crannach—*

Randal never completed the thought. In the next instant, a tumult sounded in the courtyard outside the great hall—shouting, hoofbeats, a fist pounding on the doors of the hall. Lord Alyen nodded at the doorkeeper, and the heavy double doors swung open to admit a pair of knights in armor. One of them leaned, limping, on the shoulder of the other—a younger man whom Randal recognized, after a second of disbelief, as his cousin, Walter.

And the other one . . . I've seen him before, too. Then the two men came farther into the hall, and Randal saw that the wounded man was Baron Ector of Wirrell—the same Baron Ector whom Randal had last seen at the siege of Bell Castle.

What is he doing here? Randal wondered. *He and Walter didn't exactly part friends, not after the baron accused me of stealing the gold he was keeping to pay his mercenaries.*

If the hall had been full of voices before, it was twice as noisy now. Everybody seemed to be shouting questions or giving orders, and the gray hunting dogs yelped and barked furiously at the newcomers. Randal could barely hear Walter's voice over the general racket.

"There was a battle north of here," Walter was saying. "The baron and his men against Hugo de la Corre. The baron got away with the help of his household knights, but not until the battle was lost."

"Where is de la Corre now?" Lord Alyen asked as Walter helped the baron down onto a bench near the high table.

71

"Coming south," said Walter. "A day, maybe two days, behind us." His features showed the grime and fatigue of hard riding. There were dark circles under his eyes, and his mouth was a tight line. "And he has a master wizard for his ally."

Randal leaned forward. "Do you know the name of Hugo's wizard?" he asked. *He has to be the one I saw in my vision. Why else would he have attacked Diamante twice already?*

"Randy?" Walter looked around at the sound of Randal's voice. "You made good time getting here, cousin. De la Corre's wizard is called Varnart, and I hope he isn't a friend of yours. I was at the battle, and I saw sorceries worked there that I still don't want to think about."

Varnart, thought Randal. He clenched his fists so tightly that the scar across his right palm began to ache. *Of all the master wizards in Brecelande, I have to be facing him.*

Randal drew a deep breath. "No, Walter," he said finally. "De la Corre's wizard is no friend of mine. Not since I destroyed something he wanted—an artifact of power, but an evil one. If he were using it now, I don't think there'd be any hope left. And if he knows I'm the wizard who's helping the princess, he's probably overjoyed at the chance to get revenge."

Lord Alyen frowned at Randal. "Is there anything you can do to protect the rest of us?"

Randal glanced about the hall. All the others, he realized uncomfortably, were looking at him—not as if they blamed him for bringing more danger to a castle already facing a siege, but with trusting expectation.

I have to do something, he thought again. *But nobody at the Schola was a student of magical warfare— not on Varnart's level, at least. How on earth can I defend an entire castle from a wizard's attack?*

VI.
Nightmare

RANDALL LOOKED AT his uncle in the flickering torchlight of the great hall.

"I'll do what I can," he said finally. "I'll build a magic circle around the entire castle. That should keep Master Varnart's spells away from us for a little while."

"How soon can you do it?" asked Lord Alyen.

Randal stood. "Let me borrow a spear from the armory to cut the turf with, and I'll get the circle up right now. Varnart's just had his spell turned back on him. He won't be sending magic this way again until he can work something new."

A few minutes later, Randal stood outside the closed gates of Castle Doun, looking upward at the sheer, looming walls. The night was clear and moonless, with only the burning stars to give light and to silhouette the dark shapes of towers and battlements. The size of his self-imposed task gave the young wizard pause. Doun wasn't as big as the walled city of Widsegard or Bell Castle, which had stood on Brecelande's eastern border. All the same, the thought of protecting it by his magical powers alone was a daunting one.

And the longer I stand here, he reminded himself, *the more likely it is that Master Varnart will strike again. Time to get to work.*

He set the point of the spear into the springy turf and started drawing the circle, step by step, around the walls of Doun. Cutting through the tangled mat of roots and grass was hard work, more suited to a team of oxen and a plow than to a single youth with a sharpened spearhead. Before Randal was done, his back and shoulders were sore, and his scarred hand ached as if the slash across the palm were fresh.

At last, though, he made the cut that joined the end of the circle to its beginning and stepped back a little from his handiwork. He leaned on the spear to catch his breath before going on to the next step—marking the circle with the four directions and the mystical symbols. A false dawn was already turning the sky gray in the east. As he rested, Randal saw a solitary figure coming on foot up the road to the castle gate. At the sight of the journeyman wizard, the figure halted.

"Ho there, young Randal," came a familiar voice out of the lingering darkness. A small sphere of blue-white cold-flame sprang to life in the air above the newcomer's hand, revealing the smiling, bearded face of Madoc the Wayfarer. "Is there room for one more inside your circle?"

"Master Madoc!" exclaimed Randal, starting forward. Then he hesitated. "It *is* Master Madoc, isn't it?"

The newcomer chuckled. "I'm Madoc. You can check for disguises and illusions if you want to," said the master wizard. "I won't be offended."

Randal laughed in turn, although rather shakily. "No, I'll believe it's you. But hurry inside—we've been attacked by magic once already, and I need to get the circle set before the next assault."

Madoc stepped over the line Randal had carved into the turf. "Do you know who's been attacking you?" he asked.

"I think it's a master named Varnart," Randal told him. "He's working with Hugo de la Corre—and he didn't like me even before I allied myself with the princess."

"Varnart," said Madoc. "I'm not surprised. Someday you'll have to tell me just how you happened to cross him."

"I interfered with his plans once before," said Randal. "Something he was trying to steal came to me instead, and I don't think he's forgotten it."

"Varnart always did hold grudges," the master wizard said. His expression was grim in the glow of the cold-flame. "If you've thwarted him once already, he won't rest until you're out of his way for good. And the spells of destruction were his special study."

"That's all I needed," said Randal gloomily. "A blood feud with a master of battle-magic."

"You seem to be holding your own so far," observed Madoc. "But why don't you let me finish closing the circle? I have a hunch that right now you're of more use inside the castle than out of it."

Randal gratefully handed over the spear to Master Madoc and went back into the castle. Inside the great hall, he found Walter and Lord Alyen standing together beside the bench where Baron Ector lay wounded.

"It's good you're back," Lord Alyen said as Randal joined them. "The baron's in worse shape than we thought. The village healwife tried her best, but his injuries go too deep for her magic to mend them. Walter says you can help."

Randal looked down at Baron Ector. The baron had been stripped of his armor and now wore only a plain linen undertunic. One arm had been splinted and freshly bandaged—the work of the healwife, Randal supposed—but even in the dim torchlight he could see that the broken arm wasn't what Lord Alyen had been talking about.

The baron's eyes were swollen closed under a mass of blisters, and burns covered his nose and mouth. More burns spread across the baron's neck and hands, and rose up in red welts everywhere else that his armor hadn't covered.

"What happened?" Randal asked.

"De la Corre's wizard threw a fireball at him," said Walter. "The only thing that saved him was his armor. His horse was nothing but burned meat."

I've never seen anybody throw a fireball that big,

77

thought Randal. *Madoc didn't exaggerate about Master Varnart having a liking for the destructive spells.*

"These burns look like they've gone untended for a while," Randal said aloud. "How long ago was the battle?"

"Four days . . . no, five," said Walter. "And we've been riding just ahead of de la Corre and his army ever since. We took care of him the best we could, but . . ." The knight shrugged. "None of us are healers. You are."

"I'll try my best," Randal promised.

He closed his eyes and reached out with his magical senses. *Those burns must be painful*, he thought, and he whispered the words of comfort and ease. As soon as he saw the baron relax, he went on to work the rest of the healing spell, drawing the water out of the swollen flesh and removing the poisons that had built up while the burns went untended.

At last, the baron fell into the deep sleep of healing, and Randal sat back with a sigh. Lord Alyen stood for a moment looking at Randal with an expression of respect, and then moved off, leaving Randal and Walter alone.

The young wizard turned away from the baron and glanced at his cousin. "You were with Ector's army, weren't you?" he asked. "At the battle, I mean."

"Yes," said Walter. "When I left you in search of an army, I went to him first. It was a gamble, after the way we parted at Bell Castle, but it worked. He agreed to bring his men south and swear fealty to the princess. 'Better Hugo de la Corre than no one,' he said, 'but anyone is better than de la Corre.' We were on the road here when Hugo attacked."

Randal nodded. "And we parted—how long ago?"

"Six weeks, more or less," said Walter. "Why?"

Six weeks, thought Randal. *But the time I spent riding with Ullin seemed like minutes.*

Before he could find an answer to give his cousin, the hall doors opened and Master Madoc entered. The northern wizard strode over to where Baron Ector lay sleeping, looked down at the wounded nobleman, and gave an approving nod.

"You do good work, lad," Madoc said as he joined Randal and Walter. "But now you should rest for tomorrow. The circle is up around the walls, and it should keep out Varnart's magical attacks for a while, at least."

Walter looked at Randal with a confused expression. "But when you fought the demon in Master Balpesh's tower, you broke the circle there just by touching it. How can something that fragile protect the whole castle?" He paused, and then added in lower tones, "I've seen what Varnart can do, and I don't want to watch it again here."

"This time," promised Madoc, "Varnart will have other wizards to contend with. And as for breaking the circle"—he smiled briefly—"you're confusing a barrier meant to keep something *in* with a barrier meant to keep something *out.*"

Another voice, roughened and weary, spoke

79

from the entrance to the stairway. "You always did have a knack with those."

The accent sounded familiar. Randal turned and saw Master Crannach coming into the hall. The foreign wizard's face was streaked with sweat and his skin was gray from fatigue, but he had an air of triumph about him just the same.

He sank onto a bench, pulled a flagon to him with his bandaged hand, and drained it at a gulp. Then he lowered the flagon and said to Master Madoc, "It's done. Whatever we face, it will be only the forces of men and nature, not of the lower plane, that menace us."

"What made you think about demons in the first place?" Randal asked Crannach. The wizard refilled his flagon and drank again, more slowly this time.

"Demons feed on disorder," said Crannach. "It draws them like rotting meat draws flies. And Varnart is going to be a difficult enough adversary to fight without having demons to reckon with as well."

Randal was still curious. "How did you know to come here?"

Crannach gave a faint chuckle and nodded toward Madoc. "Our footloose friend over there came to Tarnsberg last summer to give me some advice. 'A day may come,' he said, 'when the City Council and the Regents of the Schola will decide to bar the gates and tell some lord that he can look elsewhere for loyal subjects. And if the winds of the world ever blow thus,' he said, 'then go at once to Castle Doun and offer them your aid.' Not long ago, everything came to pass as he had described it—so the rest of the wizards stayed in Tarnsberg to protect the school and the city, and I came here."

Walter nodded slowly. "You talked with Master Crannach before you guided us to Elfland," the knight said to Madoc. "Did you know that de la Corre would seize the throne?"

"Predicting the future is Madoc's special gift," said Master Crannach. "When he tells me that it would be wise to do something, I pay heed."

"Well, then," said Madoc, "I can tell all of you that the best thing to do now is to go to your beds and sleep. It won't help anybody if you're exhausted when tomorrow comes."

Nobody argued with him, but finding places for everyone took a little time. The great hall and the courtyard were already filled with the peasants from Doun village and the fighting men who had come with Walter and Baron Ector. In the end, Randal accommodated himself with a pallet in a small alcove off the great hall. Normally, the little room was used as a pantry, but tonight the crockery had been cleared away to make a private place for an honored guest.

Honored guest—me, of all people. Randal smiled to himself at the thought. *I remember when I was just another of the castle squires.*

He looked about the tiny pantry. *I fetched a bowl from this very chamber when Master Madoc first came to*

Castle Doun. He used it to look into the future for everybody—everybody except me.

The memory sobered him. *Madoc promised Sir Palamon a battle that would bring him fame for the rest of his days. Is this the time?*

Randal had a sneaking suspicion that it might be. Still, he was tired. It was late, and he had worked a great deal of magic. He lay down on his pallet and relaxed as he had been taught in the Schola. Sleep came to him, but he fell into dreams —confused and contradictory images, swirling in fragments about him as he slumbered. He *was* dreaming, he knew, but he was unable to catch hold of any one dream and equally unable to wake.

Then a bolt of lightning flashed across his vision in a white sheet of blinding brightness. He gazed about wildly and saw that he stood in a dim, echoing cavern, lit only by the flickering glow of torches. The torches were borne by a train of men and women pacing in a funeral procession, with a silent form carried in their midst on a wooden bier.

Who is dead? Randal wondered. But he had no time to do more than wonder before the scene shifted, and he knew that it was he himself the marchers carried. He was lying down; he could see the torches all around him and feel the jarring bump of their pace as they bore him on the wooden slab, surrounded by heaps of flowers.

Randal looked to his right and saw Lys walking beside the procession. Her lute was smashed to kindling, and she carried it broken in her hands.

Tears streaked her face as she looked over to meet Randal's eyes.

Is she weeping for her lute, he wondered, *or for me?*

"Why did you do it?" Lys said in his dream. "Why did you fail us?"

"I didn't . . ." Randal began, but he never finished. He felt the cloth of a shroud closing over his face, dimming his sight and cutting off his breath.

He lashed out at the grave-cloth—and found it to be nothing more than the sheet on his bed. The cold light of early dawn made the alcove's narrow window-slit into a strip of gray against the black of the castle wall.

He sat up, shivering from the nightmare. *It was so real,* he thought. *Like the other dreams that came unbidden and always spoke true.* He climbed to his feet and reached for his tunic and journeyman's robe. *I have to talk with somebody about this.*

Most of the castle was still asleep. When Randal left the alcove and went out into the great hall, he had to pick his way between snoring forms wrapped in cloaks or blankets. Five years before, when he had gone looking for Master Madoc to ask to be taught magic, Randal had found him at a window in the castle's chief tower. Now Randal turned his steps that way again.

But the tower stairs were empty, and the windows looked out onto fields buried in dense fog. At the top of the tower he found not the wizard, but his cousin. Sir Walter was leaning on the chest-high parapet and looking out at the fog that covered the countryside around Doun—an expanse of dark gray stretching out to meet a pale gray sky, too dense for any details to be seen. Walter turned around as Randal came up onto the tower.

"You couldn't sleep, either?" he asked.

"I had bad dreams," said Randal.

He joined his cousin at the wall and stood gazing out at the mist. Somewhere out there, he knew, was the circle that he had drawn around Castle Doun and that Master Madoc had activated. He could sense its protective power wrapped about them, even though the circle itself was invisible.

"Bad dreams," Walter repeated. His voice sounded uneasy. "Like the dream you had before I was wounded at Tattinham?"

"Like and unlike," said Randal. "I dreamed about myself. . . . I'd failed everyone somehow, by doing something, or by not doing something . . . I'm not sure. But my dreams have a way of coming true, and now I'm afraid."

Walter gave a short laugh. "So what makes you wizards different from the rest of us?"

"Not that kind of fear," said Randal, sighing. "So much is at stake here—crowns and kingdoms and maybe the safety of the whole mortal world—and I'm standing right in the middle of it. Me, the journeyman wizard who, back in my apprentice days, couldn't even light a candle after two years of trying! How on earth am I supposed to know the right thing to do?"

"I can't tell you that," Walter answered, after a moment. "All I know is what Father told me when I left Doun to go follow the tournaments— 'Be true to your sworn word, and don't dishonor the ones who taught you.' Good advice for a knight, but for a wizard . . . I don't know, Randy. I'm sorry."

"Never mind," said Randal. "It's all right."

He and Walter stood side by side for a long while in silence, leaning on the wall and looking out over the slowly brightening landscape. The sun rose and burned the fog away. And when the fog was gone, the lowlands all around Doun were covered with the banners and tents of the army of Hugo de la Corre.

VII.
The Portal

WALTER PUSHED HIMSELF away from the parapet with a tired sigh. "Time to get myself armed and armored."

Randal nodded. "If you see Lord Alyen, tell him that, so far, the circle of protection is holding."

"How do you know?"

"I'd have felt it break," said Randal. "And besides—you can see for yourself that not even the fog came inside the boundary."

Walter headed off down the stairs. Randal stayed behind, looking out at the enemy camp. Already the sentries on the castle walls were crying the alarm, and distant shouts and trumpet calls rose up from the field outside the walls. Footsteps sounded behind him, and he turned to see his uncle and Master Madoc.

"De la Corre will be sending a herald as soon as the sun's all the way up," Lord Alyen was saying to the wizard as the two men came onto the watchtower. "I might as well be waiting."

"What are you going to tell him?" Randal asked.

"Nothing more than he's guessed already," said Lord Alyen. "Simply that Castle Doun will neither swear allegiance nor surrender." He went over to the parapet and stood leaning against the stone, much as Walter had done only a little while before. "But at least the formalities will have been observed."

Master Madoc touched Randal on the shoulder. "Randal, lad . . . there's something we need to talk about downstairs."

Puzzled, Randal followed the master wizard back down the spiral stairway. Madoc stopped outside the door of the solar. Sir Palamon stood there, fully armed, with a sword in its scabbard at his waist.

"Open the chamber door, Sir Knight," Madoc said. "Young Randal needs to see what you and I have seen."

Sir Palamon opened the door, and the three of them stepped into the solar. Randal saw the furniture standing as it had stood the day before—the table and chairs, the embroidery frames, the spindles, the baskets of wool and yarn, the loom all threaded and prepared for Lady Elene's tapestry work. Lys's lute lay forlorn beside a chair.

Trouble, Randal thought. *Lys never goes anywhere without her lute.*

"I don't see anyone here," he said.

"That's the problem," said Sir Palamon with a frown. "After the feasting last night, Lady Elene put the princess and the demoiselle from Occitania to bed here in this chamber, where the princess could have privacy befitting her station." He paused. "And I myself stood guard last night outside the chamber door."

A feeling of cold foreboding started to curl around Randal like the morning fog. The lute accused him mutely. Aloud, he said only, "I don't suppose you saw anybody entering or leaving the chamber during the night?"

Sir Palamon shook his head. "No one."

Madoc pointed at the floor in the center of the chamber. "Cast a spell of magical resonance," he said to Randal, "and direct it to that spot. Tell me what you see."

Still enveloped in his sense of foreboding, Randal obeyed. The echo from the spell of resonance—a charm designed to tell a wizard about other magicians or magical devices at work in a particular spot—nearly knocked him off his feet.

"It's a magic portal," he said, when he had recovered. "Or the traces of one, at any rate." He turned to Sir Palamon. "When did Lady Elene bring the ladies up to bed? What was I doing then?"

The master-at-arms thought for moment. "You'd just gone outside," he said finally.

Randal bit his lip. "De la Corre's wizard must have come into the castle through a portal and stolen Diamante and Lys away while I was still drawing the circle around the walls, before the protective spells were in place." He looked over at Madoc. "How much power can Varnart *have*, to work a spell like that so soon after having a major magic-working closed down in his face?"

"Varnart is very powerful," the northern wizard said. "I knew him when he was first made a master. He had enough strength even then to defeat wizards far more skilled than he."

Randal looked back to the empty space in the center of the room. "Somebody has to go after the princess and Lys." He paused. "Whoever does it is going blind through another wizard's portal, and no one knows what waits on the other side."

He paused again and looked at the stone floor. He didn't like where his thoughts were taking him. "You and Master Crannach are needed here," he continued at last. "Someone has to keep the magic circle from breaking and maintain the walls between this world and the demonic plane. If anybody goes after the princess, it should be me."

"I agree," Madoc said. "You're the one with the best chance. And the princess knows and trusts you."

For a long time, Randal was silent. *What a time,* he thought bitterly, *to have master wizards start treating me like a friend and colleague.*

"I don't like the thought of doing it alone," he said at last, "but I will."

"I'll go with you," said Sir Palamon, "if Lord Alyen gives me his leave. The loss of the princess is my fault, since she was in my keeping."

The master-at-arms hurried off. When he reappeared not long after, Sir Walter followed close behind. Like Sir Palamon, Randal's cousin was fully armored. He held a helm in one hand; in a scabbard slung down his back, he carried a massive greatsword like the one he had found and used in Bell Castle.

"Sir Palamon told me what happened," Walter said. "And there may be more than magical danger on the far side of the portal. You'll need my sword, and Sir Palamon's as well."

Randal picked up the fallen lute and held it loosely by the neck in his left hand. "Stand with me in the center of the room," he told the two knights. "I'm going to open Varnart's portal from this end." He looked over at Madoc. "If you could guard the door—just in case something nasty comes back through instead of us. . . ."

"Of course, lad." The northern wizard shut the door of the solar behind him and stood with his back against it. "That's a barrier-spell, like the circle. It'll be no trouble to keep both of those going at once."

Randal took up a position in the middle of the room and gestured at Walter and Sir Palamon to join him. *There's no way to put it off any longer,* he thought, and he murmured the words of portal-opening.

Without an amulet or talisman to anchor the spell, opening the portal was slow and difficult, like working a puzzle. As with all spells, the spirit of its maker showed in every twist and turn. Randal knew he would recognize Varnart when they met by the feel of the other wizard's power alone.

As the spell took effect, the solar faded and changed. Randal—and Walter and Sir Palamon with him—stood in a dark forest, in the midst of tall, heavy-branched trees growing among cliffs of bare rock and huge boulders. The dawn sky was only a few patches of gray showing through the green leaves overhead.

A clearing opened before them; five cut stones pointed into the sky. Between the stones stood two wooden stakes. Five men lay on the ground, swords fallen from their hands.

Randal went forward, with Walter and Sir Palamon close behind. He bent over one of the fallen men. The man's clothing confirmed what he already knew—this was one of the men in Master Varnart's pay. Randal looked up as Walter and Sir Palamon joined him.

"He's one of Varnart's," the young wizard said. "I met others like him outside Cingestoun once. And he's been knocked out by magic, but what kind I'm not sure of. Nothing Schola-trained, so it can't be Varnart's work."

"Look over there," Walter said quietly, nodding toward one of the two wooden poles. "What do you make of that?"

The knight pointed at a pair of rings attached to the top of the pole. Two ropes lay on the ground, and beside them rested a scrap of green silk.

"That cloth came from Diamante's dress," said

Randal with growing fear. "Whoever captured her and Lys brought them here and tied them up. These fellows lying on the ground were guards. What happened next, I can't be sure."

"Do you think Demoiselle Lys and the princess are still alive?" Walter asked.

"A living heir can always be made dead later if need be," Sir Palamon replied. "A dead one can't come back to life."

Randal nodded slowly in agreement. "I think our friend Varnart was trying to get an advantage over Hugo de la Corre, and the true princess was his playing piece."

But what about Lys? he wondered to himself. *What did she have to protect her? No royal rank, and Varnart probably likes her as little as he does me.*

"What do we do now?" inquired Walter. "If Varnart planned to use the princess against Hugo, something's happened to change the game."

"I'm going to try a spell," Randal said. "Lys used the lute to make her music. The two of them are bound." He held up the lute and spoke the words of a musical spell over it, a variant of the charm he sometimes used to accompany Lys when she sang and played for an audience.

As soon as he felt the spell snap closed he lifted the lute above his head. With his eyes shut, he turned on his heel. The lute began to sound, humming with a low, steady note as the bass string vibrated by itself. Randal felt a surge of relief. Lys was still alive.

He kept on turning, and the sound grew louder and more insistent. Then it started to fade. Randal turned back again, slowly, until the sound was once more at its loudest point. He opened his eyes and looked in the direction where the neck of the lute pointed.

"That way," he said.

"But I don't see any tracks going off in that direction," Sir Palamon protested.

"Just the same," said Randal, "that's the way we need to go."

The three headed out, the two knights with swords at the ready, and Randal holding the humming lute before him. He walked straight forward, in the direction that produced the loudest tone.

They had not gone far into the woods when a crowd of foul creatures leaped from the underbrush. Randal was unable to tell whether the things were men wearing hairy pelts for clothing, or some kind of beast that walked upright and howled words in an unknown tongue. The two knights whirled into action, the blades of their swords sweeping out in deadly arcs in the shadows under the trees. The strange creatures dissolved suddenly into the drifting mist. *Illusions?* Randal wondered.

From the top of a broken crag, a man laughed. "Excellent sword work," he said. "Very impressive."

The echo of the man's power was unmistakable. "Master Varnart," said Randal.

"I see you recognize me," the older wizard replied, and he bowed.

So this is Varnart, thought Randal. *He's the wizard I saw in my vision—and the one who attacked Castle Doun last night, as well. No mistake about it—this is a powerful wizard.*

Indeed, Master Varnart looked the part of a strong and dangerous master wizard. His flowing robes were cut from heavy deep blue velvet and embroidered in gold and silver threads with mystic signs that sparkled with their own inner light. His beard was long, and snow-white hair fell to his shoulders.

At the master wizard's right arm stood the princess Diamante, and on his left stood Lys. The lute-player looked as if she were boiling with anger but determined not to show it. The princess looked proud, but sad.

Varnart took a step forward into the air. He floated easily to the ground, the princess and Lys floating with him, and came to a gentle stop directly in front of the three from Castle Doun.

Before Randal could act, Varnart raised a warning hand. "Cast no spells, boy. At the first touch of your magic, the princess and her companion die. Meanwhile, let us dispose of your pair of heroes. Watch."

A rustling in the dried leaves behind Randal announced the arrival of the five men-at-arms from the clearing with the standing stones. Palamon and Walter took positions back-to-back, while the five swordsmen circled them. Palamon was closest to where Randal stood watching. Two men faced him directly, and a third was still circling to attacking position.

One moment the castle's master-at-arms was as motionless as a statue. In the next he lashed out with his sword, catching the man to his right on the inside of his left thigh. The man cried out, staggering, and went down onto his knees.

Palamon didn't hesitate. As part of the same motion, his sword came around over his head, hit the left side of his second adversary's shield, then rebounded and swung around to smash into the man's right side before he could block. The man was still falling when Palamon pivoted again, back to the man he had crippled. The master-at-arms brought his sword over and down onto the wounded man's helm, splitting it open. The man pitched forward and lay silent and still.

The master-at-arms took a pace toward the third man who had faced him, but the man fell before he could reach him. Walter's greatsword had caught him in the side of the neck. The two men who had faced Walter at the beginning of the fight lay one across the other on the ground, and their blood welled out from the gashes in their armor.

Walter and Palamon turned as one toward Varnart and lunged forward. Walter's greatsword swept down, and Palamon's blade circled in from the right at waist level. But neither connected. The swords passed through empty air. The master wizard had vanished, leaving Diamante and Lys behind.

"Quickly!" Randal said. "Back to the clearing. I need to find the portal."

The five moved out through the woods, retracing the path that Randal and the two knights had taken.

"I don't know about this," Walter said, pushing aside a branch. "If this is really an escape, it seems too easy."

"He's letting us go," agreed Sir Palamon.

"But why?" Lys asked.

"Let's not stay to find out," said Randal as they came to the place where the portal had been. "Everyone join hands," he instructed, and he chanted the words of the portal-opening.

We're safe as long as Master Madoc is still keeping his end open. . . .

The world swirled before his eyes, and the trees reformed into the interior of the solar, where Master Madoc still stood with his back to the door.

"You've done well," Madoc said. "But Her Highness is needed on the walls. We don't have much time."

Randal and the others followed Madoc up the spiral stairway at a run. When they reached the top of the tower, Randal saw that Lord Alyen was still standing there, looking out at the camp of the besiegers. Randal joined him by the parapet.

"Has de la Corre sent out his herald?" the young wizard asked.

"Not yet," said Lord Alyen. "But he will soon, I think."

A horn blew far off in the field beyond the castle, and a small party of mounted men rode up the hill toward Doun. One of them carried the banner of Hugo de la Corre—a huge raven, its wings outstretched in flight. Another wore the blank white surcoat of a herald. They rode up to the limits of the magic circle. The invisible boundary flared up briefly with blue light when the lead horse touched it. The creature reared and refused to go farther.

"All you in the castle," the herald called. "If you will surrender the girl and swear fealty to King Hugo, we will depart in peace."

Diamante stepped forward before Lord Alyen could speak. She mounted up onto the parapet, where all those below could see her, and stood with her long silver hair unbound and whipping out behind her like a banner in the wind.

"If the pretender desires peace, let him go back to his own lands," she cried, in a voice that carried over tower and field. "But I am the true and rightful queen, and it is *you* who must swear allegiance to *me*."

VIII.

The Fighting on the Walls

NO OTHER REPLY came from the castle. Lord Alyen himself stepped up to the flagstaff, tied on the banner the princess had brought with her from Elfland, and hauled it up to fly above the banner of Castle Doun.

"That should give them something to think about," he said as the blue and silver banner with its leaping deer and kingly crown floated above them. The riders outside the magic circle turned their horses and rode back the way they had come. Diamante stood beside Lord Alyen, looking out at the enemy camp. After a little while, Master Madoc turned away from them and left the tower.

Randal hesitated, glancing from his uncle and the princess to the stairway where Madoc had gone. Then he went after the master wizard. Lys came with him. Together they descended the wooden stairs that wound around the outside of the watchtower and went out onto the battlements of Castle Doun. There the master wizard paced along the walls in silence, seeming not to heed the curious glances of the archers and men-at-arms.

From the feel of magic in the air and the look of concentration on Madoc's face, Randal knew that the northern wizard was testing the strength of his protective circle. Randal and Lys went with him all the way around the castle walls, while down below in the besieger's camp, drums began to beat. Mixed with the drums came the high, bright notes of trumpets and the low, whooping voices of the battle horns.

Varnart has to attack soon, Randal thought. *He and de la Corre don't have time to sit outside the walls and wait for Castle Doun's food and water to run out. Hugo has to be at the Field of Kings by Midsummer's Day.*

Lys looked nervously out at the field. The morning sun shone down on a host of wooden siege engines—trebuchets for throwing heavy boulders over or against the stone walls of Doun, battering rams to break down the gates, tall wooden scaling towers that stood as high as the castle's parapets.

"Wouldn't we be safer inside?" she asked Randal.

Master Madoc halted in his pacing and looked at her over his shoulder. "While the circle is in place, we're as safe up here as we would be anywhere else." The northern wizard smiled a little. "Although our friend Crannach would say it was the barbarian in me, I've always preferred to do my fighting out in the open air."

And fighting there would be, Randal knew.

Before any of the war engines down below could be brought against the walls of Castle Doun, the circle he and Madoc had worked to put into place would have to be broken.

And that means wizard going against wizard, he thought. *Master Varnart against Madoc and Crannach . . . and me. Three of us should be enough to keep the circle unbroken—but Madoc was right when he said that Varnart is a wizard of enormous power.*

He glanced over at Lys. "How did Master Varnart capture you and Diamante, anyway?" he asked. "And just what *did* happen to the guards at the standing stones?"

"It was strange," said the girl. "We were back in the solar and I was tuning my lute, when something I couldn't quite see reached out of nowhere and snatched up the princess. I made a grab for her and off we went together. Next thing I knew, we were in the clearing and tied against those stakes."

She paused for a moment, as if remembering, and then went on. "After a while, the wizard showed up."

"Varnart," said Randal.

Lys's blue eyes widened. "So that's who it was! After what you did to that ivory statue of his, no wonder he was so happy at the thought of doing you harm! He gloated a bit and told Diamante that she shouldn't fear for her safety, since she was more valuable alive than dead. 'A whip to keep Hugo in line,' he called her. He didn't have anything nearly as comforting to say to me, I can tell you—I thought I was done for. 'But where you go,' he told me, 'that meddling youngster is sure to follow . . . which pleases me very well.' "

Once again, Randal felt a sense of foreboding. *Varnart's a wizard,* he thought, *and he likes his power too much to corrupt it by lying. Magic changed the world, and the world is made of truth. No one who lies can expect to command the truth. If Varnart said my coming pleased him, then he meant it. But then why did he let me go?*

"Anyway," Lys continued, "Varnart left, and the men you saw there started to mock us, laughing, bowing down to the princess and asking her to command them. Then, all at once, they fell asleep and lay on the ground snoring."

Master Madoc nodded. "I know that spell," he said. "The princess must have learned it in the Fair Realm. Elfin magic in mortal hands is slow but sure. What happened next?"

"Well," Lys replied, "the ropes fell away from us—another spell, I think. Then we went looking for an elf-fort, but Varnart found us. He froze us to the ground so that we couldn't lift our feet. He said we'd wait for our friends to come find us. So we did. And you know the rest."

For a while there was silence as the three stood looking out at the field of tents. Armed men emerged from the camp, sunlight flashing on their weapons. They clustered together around the banners and battle-standards. More drums and trumpets added their noises to the sounds below. On the walls and towers of the castle, familiar voices called out orders—Walter and Lord Alyen, Sir Palamon and Sir Iohan, reminding the archers and spearmen to keep still, lest an arrow or a javelin coming from the castle walls break the magic circle's protection from the inside. Diamante also walked along the walls, and wherever she passed, men stood straighter and looked more hopeful.

The men of de la Corre's army came up the hill toward Castle Doun, but they slowed and stopped before they reached the circle's unseen boundary. The magical barrier was still in place: A stone flung from a trebuchet arced up toward the castle, only to rebound from the air and fall among the men who ringed the base of the hill.

Randal heard Lys breathe a sigh of relief. His own hands had clenched so tightly into fists that it hurt to open them—not because he had doubted the strength of Madoc's protective circle, but because for the first time he fully understood what was happening. War had come to Castle Doun.

He looked out at the distant landscape, away from the fighting men and siege engines closer to the castle walls. A small cloud floated on the western horizon. As Randal watched, the cloud grew with unnatural speed. It towered upward and spread into an enormous flattened anvil that darkened the hillside underneath.

"Ah," said Madoc, following his gaze. "It begins.

And now we see whose magic is the strongest."

"Where's Master Crannach?" Lys asked. "Isn't he going to help you?"

"He is already helping us," said Madoc, "by keeping watch over the barriers against the demonic plane." The master wizard smiled again, briefly. "He'll be locked away in his chamber by now. Crannach is a man who likes his comfort, and he works indoors whenever he can."

"Good for him," said Lys. She bit her lip and glanced unhappily at the sky. "But I think the rest of us are going to get rained on."

Randal had to agree. Off in the west, a whole line of tall, anvil-headed clouds had joined the first one. They advanced rapidly over the rolling hills, blotting out the sun and throwing the whole countryside into darkness. Along the storm front, lightning cracked and thunder rolled. A hot wind swirled across the top of the battlements, bringing a feeling of magic in the air—magic strong and sure, but with a will of destruction behind it that made Randal shiver.

Varnart isn't even pretending to be subtle in his attack, he realized. *Does he think so little of us?*

As if in answer to his thought, a crown of lightning flashed above the towers of Castle Doun. Then the storm wind came and swept along the battlements, filling the hot air with dust and leaves. The magical barrier began to glow a dull red all around and above the castle. White rays, like lightning bolts frozen in time or the roots of a monstrous plant, squirmed over the transparent shield.

A humming sound filled the air. The white patterns writhed faster. On the castle wall, Master Madoc stood without moving; his eyes were closed and his features wrapped in deep concentration. Even without casting a spell of resonance, Randal could feel the echoes of the master wizard's power as Madoc held the protective circle against Varnart's magical assault.

"What's happening?" Lys demanded.

"We're being attacked," Randal said. "Those white patterns are Varnart trying to break our circle from outside."

Then one of the men-at-arms standing nearby gave a strangled shout and raised his arm to fling a javelin out over the wall into the surrounding army.

"No!" cried Randal.

He threw a shock-spell at the man, knocking the javelin away before it could fly outward and break the circle. Lys dove for the weapon and snatched it up before the man could reach it.

Randal left her holding the javelin and went over to the man who had tried to throw it. "Why did you do that?" he demanded. "Didn't Sir Palamon or Lord Alyen warn you about breaking the magic circle?"

The man was pale, and his breath came fast. He had the look of a horse just before it bolts. "Can't you see them?" he asked, and he pointed a shaky finger outward. "Skeletons and snakes, climbing up the walls!"

Randal looked where the man was pointing, but he saw nothing. Frowning, he cast the spell of magical resonance. The echo of magic came back to him, a complex illusion aimed at the unwizardly, which bore the unmistakable stamp of Varnart's power.

"They're not real!" he shouted, his voice carrying to all the men around him. "None of it is real!"

He could hear other voices taking up the cry— Palamon's, Walter's, Lord Alyen's—and the defenders along the wall steadied again.

But the spell of illusion shouldn't have been working at all. Randal cast the spell of resonance again, this time at the circle itself. The magical barrier was still in place and stronger than ever with the energy Master Madoc was pouring into it. *This is impossible. Varnart is sending an illusion through an unbroken circle!*

Then understanding came to him, cold and clear. *Varnart isn't sending it in through the circle. He sent it back through the portal with me, before the assault even started.*

Randal laughed bitterly at himself. *And I had the arrogance to call the man strong without being subtle. The whole point of taking Lys and Diamante must have been to slip an illusion-spell through Madoc's defenses!*

The young wizard began to hurry along the walls. *I don't dare try to break the illusion,* he thought. *I might break the shield as well.* "Don't look at those things," he said over and over to the defenders. "De la Corre's wizard is trying to trick you. Don't look!"

Then Randal looked over the edge of the wall himself. A man was crawling out of the castle gate, making his way inch by inch across the open ground between the castle and the magical barrier. Drawn by an illusion that Randal couldn't see, the man had almost reached his goal—he raised his arm up and stretched out his hand toward the red-glowing circle.

Randal threw another shock-spell, this time at the crawling man down below. But it was too late. The man's hand touched the magical barrier and pushed through. The circle burst like a soap bubble, and the red colors and the shifting lights vanished as if they had never been.

There was a shout from outside the castle. De la Corre's army rushed up in a clamor of war cries and trumpets, and javelins from catapults and stones from trebuchets spun through the air above the walls.

"Randal, lad!"

It was Madoc's voice. Randal turned and saw the master wizard leaning against the castle wall, as if the breaking of the circle had struck him like a blow. Lys stood beside him, still grasping the rescued javelin in one hand. Randal ran back along the wall to join them.

"Master Madoc!" he exclaimed. "Are you all right?"

The master wizard straightened up. "I'll do well enough," he said. "But now run and fetch Master Crannach—the three of us together can cast a protective spell even Varnart can't break."

Randal hurried back to the watchtower and the inner stairway leading down into the main part of the castle. Lys hesitated a moment and then ran after him, the javelin still in her hand. When Randal came to the chamber where Crannach had been staying, he hammered on the door with his clenched fist.

"Master Crannach!" he shouted as he knocked. "Madoc needs you on the walls!"

The simple locking-spell gave way at his touch as it had the night before. The door swung open and Randal went inside. A few steps into the room he stopped.

Master Crannach lay sprawled on the stone floor in the middle of his circle. The blood-red markings around the circle glowed like living fire. Randal saw new, stronger characters written among them, making a barrier sealed against demonic attack by that strongest of all magic, a wizard's blood. Crannach's skin was pale and clammy, and he tried in vain to rise as Randal and Lys knelt on the floor beside him.

"Tell my friend Madoc . . . I'm sorry," Crannach said. His voice was faint and thready. "I've reached the . . . end of my strength. No more . . ."

"You've locked this world to the demons," Randal said. "It is enough."

Crannach shook his head. "A false king . . . the whole world's at risk. . . ." His eyelids drifted shut, then snapped open again. "The princess . . . you will stand beside her?"

"While I live," Randal promised quietly. "Rest now."

He stood up again. Taking Lys by the sleeve, he drew her with him out of the chamber and closed the door behind him. Then he laid his hand on the wood and cast a spell of visible illusion to make the door appear the same to the touch and sight as the cut stone of the rest of the passageway.

"Why did you do that?" Lys asked.

"To hide him," said Randal, "in case Hugo takes the castle."

Lys stopped. She stood in the center of the stairway and looked at him. "You really think Castle Doun is going to fall, don't you?"

Randal met her eyes. "Yes," he said. "We're out-numbered, and Varnart is a powerful master of war-magic. I've felt his touch already, and I don't think even Madoc can equal him in his chosen field."

The lute-player swallowed and tightened her grip on the javelin. Already her knuckles were white from the pressure. "What are we going to do?" she asked.

"You've got to save yourself while you have a chance," Randal said. "Go to the elf-fort. I'll take you to the postern gate and give you a disguise that'll help you pass unnoticed."

Lys's blue eyes had been dark with fear. At his

words they blazed up with sudden anger. "And just what," she demanded, "are you going to do once I'm safely on my way?"

He shrugged. "Help Master Madoc for as long as I can—then try to get Diamante to safety."

"But you want to send me away now." The lute-player's skin was almost bone-white with anger, and her voice trembled. "After all we've seen together, do you really take me for that much of a coward?"

Randal shook his head, feeling very tired. "No," he said. "Never that. But you shouldn't have to die because of my failures."

"I'm here of my own free will," Lys said firmly. "And while you stay, I stay."

Randal sighed. "Find Diamante and stick with her. If the castle falls, we'll try to get out together."

"Right," she said. She stood looking at him for a moment, then gave him a quick, awkward hug and ran off, still carrying the javelin in one hand.

Randal stood for a moment longer, and then went on down the stairs and out through the great hall into the courtyard. The yard was full of lashing rain coming down from the green-black clouds. Through the downpour, Randal could see that the great main gate of Castle Doun was shut and barred—as was the small side gate—but the attackers pounded and shouted beyond the walls.

I might as well do what I can here, he thought, *before I go back to Master Madoc.*

Quickly he put spells of closure and locking on both the main gate and the smaller one. As he did so, he heard a shout from the south wall—Palamon's voice, yelling something that sounded like "Push them away! Push them away!"

Scaling ladders, thought Randal. *De la Corre's men are trying to get onto the walls.*

Then a steady booming noise blended with the thunder from the skies, and Randal saw the gate rock and sway on its hinges as a battering ram struck again and again. A round boulder, thrown by a trebuchet, came over the castle walls on a high, looping path. It smashed into the wall near where Randal stood. There was a crack of splintering stone, and sharp-edged rock fragments flew everywhere. One granite shard grazed Randal's cheek, drawing blood. He felt the warm fluid running down his face, mixing with the cold rainwater that still poured down from the storm-wracked clouds overhead.

A cold feeling grew in Randal's belly. *They're attacking my home,* he thought, *where I grew up.*

Just then a crack louder than the loudest thunder echoed through the courtyard, and a shock passed through the stones beneath his feet. At the same time, the livid blue-white glare of Varnart's magic lit up the top of the wall above and beside the gates. The gatehouse collapsed in a pile of broken stone, and the knights and foot soldiers of Hugo de la Corre came climbing over the rubble and into the open courtyard of Castle Doun.

IX.

Enemy Within the Gates

FOR NO LONGER than it took to draw a single, unbelieving breath, Randal stood and stared at the invaders. Then, with a wordless outcry, he called his power to him and threw a shock-spell at the foremost of de la Corre's knights. The blow knocked the man off his feet and sent him flying backward, toppling two more of his comrades with him.

More knights and foot soldiers came forward over the rubble, all of them wearing de la Corre's raven on their surcoats. Randal threw the shock-spell again and again, holding back their advance while the peasants and foot soldiers of Doun retreated into the great hall. He knew that any minute now Varnart would realize what he was doing and stop him.

Randal laughed aloud—a noise that shocked him with the ragged note of hysteria in it. *Master Varnart isn't just going to "stop" you,* he reminded himself, even while he sent a wall of illusory flame blazing high into the air in front of de la Corre's advancing knights. *He's going to kill you outright. And that's the end of all your hopes. You'll never reach mastery now.*

The unreal flames he'd thrown into the middle of the courtyard burned higher and higher. The men in raven surcoats retreated. Then somebody farther back in the press shouted, "Keep on going! It isn't real!" and once again the mass of men surged forward.

A ball of red-orange fire smashed down onto the flagstones of the courtyard in the midst of his wall of flame. *Varnart?* thought Randal. But his own illusory fire did not die, only grew brighter, and the first man to reach that burning barrier screamed when it touched his flesh.

Another fireball came blazing down. Randal looked upward, toward the source, and saw Master Madoc standing on the castle wall. All around the northern wizard, the ramparts glowed with blue-white heat, so that Castle Doun seemed crowned with a shifting, changing halo of light. Then an arrow flew up from outside the walls—an arrow tipped and feathered in sickly green witchlight and moving with an accuracy no common bow could give.

Too late, Randal's shout of "Madoc!" echoed off the stones of the castle. The magical dart buried itself shaft-deep in Madoc's side. The master wizard tottered and fell from sight.

With Madoc's fall, the flame in the courtyard

became merely an illusion once more, and the knights of de la Corre rushed forward. The last of the courtyard's defenders retreated before them into the hall.

Randal let himself be dragged unresisting with the crowd. Seeing Madoc go down had left him momentarily stunned. The northern wizard had always seemed like Castle Doun itself, one of the unbreakable, unchangeable things in a world filled with conflict. Now, in the space of a few minutes, both were gone.

Inside the great hall, everything was noise and confusion. Men-at-arms and village folk together lay wounded or dying all around. Lady Elene, pale but calm, was shepherding the women and children out of the hall in the direction of the castle's cellars, where they would wait out the battle.

Everyone else who could still move was getting ready to help in the fighting, putting on arms and armor and taking up weapons. Randal recognized Baron Ector among the defenders. The baron was pale and weak-looking from his recent healing, but he wore his mail coat and gripped a sword in one burly fist.

At the far end of the hall where the high table had been, Lys and Diamante moved close together. Lys had her lute slung over her back by its carrying-strap, and she still carried the javelin she'd picked up off the castle wall. Diamante walked among the wounded, kneeling from time to time to place her hand on a brow or speak words of comfort. The princess looked as she always did, calm and faintly sad. Randal wondered whether she regretted leaving the Fair Realm for the mortal world.

He put the thought from him and looked about the hall for more familiar faces. Walter and Lord Alyen were nowhere in sight. Neither was Sir Palamon, but Sir Iohan was there, ordering the men-at-arms to fetch the benches and trestle tables and pile them against the door.

"Axes!" the old knight shouted at one of the squires Randal had seen the evening before. "Go to the armory and bring out spears and axes!"

The squire scurried off. Sire Iohan turned to Randal and blinked as if seeing him for the first time. "Where's Master Madoc?" he demanded. "And that foreign wizard?"

Randal clenched his fists as if the pain in his scarred hand could make him forget the image of Master Madoc transfixed by the fiery green arrow.

"Madoc's down," he said shortly. "Maybe dead. And Crannach's drained himself to exhaustion trying to protect us. If you want a wizard, I'm all that's left."

"Just help us hold the door," said Sir Iohan. "That's all I ask."

As the old knight spoke, Randal heard the first deep, shuddering boom of a battering ram swinging against the barred doors of the great hall. In desperation, he once again cast the locking-spell, but he knew it wouldn't hold for long. Magic would keep the iron bar in place, but that didn't matter—not when the battering ram alone could rip the whole door off its hinges. And he didn't even want the think about what Varnart's magic had done to the gatehouse.

Another deep, wooden-throated boom made the door shiver and groan under the impact.

You have to do something, he told himself, *before the door breaks and you see hand-to-hand combat right here in the hall.*

He stepped closer to the door. Behind him, he half-heard Sir Iohan ordering the squires and the men-at-arms into a shield-wall. Most of his attention, though, was fixed on the door. The men with the ram were just on the other side, where they could swing back the heavy beam of wood and then let its own weight help slam it forward.

Fear and confusion, he thought. *Let their own evil intentions come back at them and hasten their flight.*

The ram struck again. Randal raised his arms.

"*Imago terroris,*" he called out in the Old Tongue. "*Imago malevolentiae—fiat!*"

The pounding stopped.

They've retreated for a little while, thought Randal, *but that's not enough. I have to do something else that will keep them away.*

He quickly cast the spell of heat on the stones of the doorway and the stairs outside. Within seconds, they began to glow a bright, pulsing red. Randal heard noises—shouts and screams mixed with a few oaths—and then there was a long and deadly silence. Even the unwizardly in the great hall could feel it. The squires and men-at-arms in the shield-wall glanced at each other uneasily; Baron Ector and Sir Iohan stood scowling, one at either end of the line.

For Randal, the sense of powerful magic gathering slowly, inescapably, was almost impossible to bear. Then Varnart struck, and once again the stone of Castle Doun shattered in a blaze of blue-white light.

The whole front wall fell away in a cloud of dust and broken stone, and a swarm of the fiery green arrows sped into the room. One of the arrows whistled past Randal's ear. Another sank into the flesh of Sir Iohan's throat. The old knight gave a gurgling cry and crumpled to the floor.

"Steady!" Randal heard Baron Ector shouting to the men-at-arms. "Steady on! You, wizard—get the princess up into the tower, and bar the door behind you. We'll hold them off down here as long as we can."

Randal turned away from the broken door, and the shield-wall parted to let him through. He ran to the far end of the hall, where Lys and Diamante still stood waiting together.

"Guide me," the princess said.

"This way," Randal told her. Once they were through the door that led to the spiral stairway, Randal closed the door and cast a locking-spell on it. *That won't stand against Varnart's magic,* he thought as they ran on up the stairs, *or even hold out for long against an ordinary ram. But it may buy us some time when we need it.*

Halfway up the stairs, they met Walter coming down. The knight had blood on his armor and surcoat, and all along his drawn sword. The shield he carried on his left arm was cut and battered around its rim. His face was pale and smeared with dirt and sweat.

"Where are you three going?" he demanded hoarsely, as soon as he reached them. "De la Corre's men are up on the walls. Father told me to find the princess and take her to safety through the postern gate."

Randal shook his head. "It won't work. We can't reach the postern—de la Corre's got the courtyard and the hall, too."

Walter's shoulders sagged. "Then it was all for nothing," he said. "I didn't want to abandon the fighting on the walls, but Father made me go. And now—"

The princess reached out and touched Walter lightly on the wrist. "Don't despair, Sir Knight," she murmured. She turned to Randal. "The gateway in the solar. You've tasted the fruits of Elfland and see with sharper eyes than most mortals. Is your sight keen enough to take the portal and make it into a way out of this place?"

"It's not sight that I need," Randal said, "but skill to take a master wizard's spell and turn it to my own use."

"You have to try, Randy," said Walter. "There's no other way out—and I promised Father."

Lord Alyen might well be dead by now, Randal realized. His uncle would never have sent Walter away while there was still hope that the defenders could hold the castle—Walter would surely know that. Randal looked at his cousin with sudden understanding. *Walter's trying to carry out his father's last wish. Nothing else could possibly have made him leave the walls.*

"All right," Randal said to Diamante. "We'll take our chances with Varnart's portal."

They went back up the stairway to Lady Elene's solar. The noises of battle came to them from both above and below, even through the thick stone walls. *At least there's still noise to hear,* Randal told himself. *Doun's not so easy to take as Hugo and Varnart thought.*

He opened the door to the solar. The room was full of red, murky light streaming in through the tall windows. At first he thought of magic, some new and deadly spell of Master Varnart's, and then he realized that what he saw were flames, rising up in orange and yellow and bloody crimson against the black, wind-torn sky beyond the windows. The wooden stairway that led around the outside of the tower was burning.

"Everyone's retreated from the walls up to the watchtower," Walter explained, "and they've set fire to the stairway behind them."

The knight was pale and tight-lipped. Randal

didn't blame him. Once de la Corre's men won the great hall, the defenders atop the watchtower would be attacked from below as well as in front.

I'll get Lys and the princess to safety if I can, he promised himself. *And then I'll come back and . . . come back and do what? Ask de la Corre to stop the attack? Don't be stupid. Come back and do something, anyway. But I have to rework a master wizard's portal first.*

Randal cast the spell of magical resonance, and once again his newly sharpened sight picked out the ghostly outline of a magic circle on the solar floor. *I can't open the portal as it is,* he thought, *or we'll land right back in Varnart's trap. I need to redraw the circle with the proper markings.*

He cast a quick glance around the red-lit solar. *Aunt Elene uses chalk to mark up cloth for cutting. Maybe there's some in her workbasket.* He took the lump of white chalk he found and began tracing over the faint lines on the floor.

"We'll try for Tarnsberg," he said to the others as he worked. "It's the safest place I know of and the only place where we might find help."

He inscribed the last of the magical symbols around the outside of the circle. Then he stepped into the center and gestured at the others to join him. They did so—Lys and Diamante eagerly, Walter with barely concealed reluctance—and Randal began to speak the words of portal-opening.

As before, the spell was hard to work without a

material key. This time, though, he knew the peculiar feel of Varnart's power. It made him quicker at slipping his own mind into the patterns of Varnart's spell-working. The hard part would come when he tried to weave his own intentions into the fabric, turning the portal aside from its original destination and directing it toward Tarnsberg instead.

He felt the power of the spell building up within him, power drawn from his own inner reserves. Randal sensed the shape and goal of Varnart's magic begin to shift.

"Aperite portae!" he called out in the Old Tongue, and the portal opened.

I've done it, he thought, as the walls and furniture of the solar shifted and stretched like molten wax. *It's really working.*

Then, without warning, Varnart's full power came down on him with crushing force, as it had during his scrying attempt in this same chamber. Desperately, Randal tried to hold on to the spell. Anything was better than letting the portal deliver them into Varnart's grasp. Magic twisted and writhed around the circle like tongues of lightning. Varnart pulled hard, but Randal fought back with all his strength.

Then the contact with Varnart snapped. The solar chamber seemed to fall down and away from Randal, and the portal closed behind him. With a sudden jolt, his feet settled on hard ground.

He looked about, expecting to see the narrow

121

streets and wooden houses of Tarnsberg. Instead, he stood with his friends in a place where low clouds glowed a sullen red above a forest of ancient trees. A hot rush of wind swirled around him, bringing with it a thick, acrid smell.

Randal coughed and his eyes watered. He blinked them clear again and tried to focus. This time, he saw that he and the others stood near a gnarled and twisted tree that grew apart from the others in the woods—a tree that was really three trees grown together, an oak, an ash, and a rowan. Axe marks, weathered and long grown over, marred the rowan's trunk. The three trees had sprung up in a single spot and twined together until they stood as one.

I've been here before, Randal thought. *I've been here, and I remember* . . . Then, between one breath and the next, there came to him the true knowledge of what Varnart had done, and with it came a wave of sickening fear. *There are some things worse than being dead, and I've found one of them.*

"This isn't Tarnsberg," said Lys.

Walter gave a harsh laugh. "I've never been there," the knight said. "But looking at this place, I believe you."

Randal tore his gaze away from the threefold tree and met the wary eyes of his companions. "We aren't even in Brecelande," he acknowledged. "Varnart felt the portal opening and twisted the spell aside."

Diamante looked at him. "Tell them the whole

122

truth, wizard," she said. "We are no longer in the mortal world."

Randal bit his lip. "Yes," he admitted. "Varnart has sent us to the demonic plane." He bowed his head. "I'm sorry, Walter. My dream of failure has come true, after all. I meant to bring you to safety, not put you in worse danger than before."

"Isn't there any way out?" asked Lys.

Randal looked up again. "There is one chance," he said to the lute-player. "It's dangerous, but it's our only hope. Lend me your knife."

Lys frowned. "What for?"

"To cut the marks," he said. "Just stand still. And whatever you do, don't leave the circle."

Walter looked suspicious. "You said Master Crannach had put a barrier between this place and Brecelande."

"He did," said Randal. "But he built it against demons, not against mortals. Maybe I can get around his barrier and make a link between our world and here. If this works."

A motion in the forest caught Randal's eye. A vague shape was drifting between the trees. "We're being watched by demons right now. I need to get a circle up." He held out his hand. "Please, Lys—the knife."

Wordlessly, she held it out to him. Randal took it and began to construct a pair of magic circles, the most careful he had ever built. Gripping the knife awkwardly in his scarred hand, first he laid out a circle so small that only one person could fit inside it. He left that circle empty. *An inner circle to trap Varnart, and an outer circle to protect us all.* He drew the second, larger circle around both the small circle he had just drawn and the patch of dry ground where he and his friends stood close together.

The moving shapes in the forest—there were more than one—drifted closer.

Carefully, he wrote words and mystic symbols around the larger outer circle, the one that would keep the demons away. Around the inside circle he marked only the four directions. Then he stepped over the outside boundary. He now stood with his three friends inside the circle of protection and outside of the inner circle.

"Stay together," Randal said, "and be ready. Master Varnart made a mistake when he linked me to him as a way to break the defense of Doun. Now I'm going to use that link to summon him to me and force him to create another portal from our own world to this one. When he does that, the way home will open for us."

He looked at the others. "To compel a master wizard takes the most powerful of magic, the kind of power that comes only from a wizard's blood. So whatever you do, don't break the circle and let the demons feed. Once they've tasted a wizard's blood, not even Master Crannach's barriers may be strong enough to hold them away from Brecelande."

Randal's friends stood silent in the circle beside him under the branches of the threefold tree. He paused for a moment, gathering his magical powers—and his courage—to him. Then he took the knife he still held in his right hand and drew it across his left palm in a sudden jerk.

Blood sprang out in the track of the knife. The red drops fell onto the ground at his feet, and around the circle, demons gathered. Tall, slender, inhumanly beautiful, with skin like opals or mother-of-pearl, they pressed around the borders of his circle and bared their needle-sharp ivory teeth.

"Wizard," said one. Even its voice was beautiful, like the chiming of distant bells. "Little wizard. Do you know me?"

The open slash across Randal's left hand throbbed and burned. The blood was running freely now, making a red puddle in the dirt. He looked out across the barrier of his circle—strong enough to keep out demons. He'd made certain of that before he started.

"I know you," he said. "Your name is Eram, and I fought you once before, in Master Balpesh's tower."

The demon laughed, a silvery trill of music. "I almost had your blood that day."

Randal turned away from the demons. If the next spell worked, he would not have to deal with them much longer. He bent down and dipped a finger into the pool of blood that had formed at his feet. With the red liquid he marked symbol after symbol around the circle he had cut into the earth.

125

Then he drew a deep breath and began the chant that would force a master wizard to his will.

It was hard, harder by far than any spell he had ever tried. But he was succeeding. He could feel the link between them coming into existence at his command—and in spite of what had to happen next, he felt the beauty and satisfaction of a perfectly made spell singing in his blood like music.

Randal spoke the final syllables of his spell, and the characters he'd drawn around the magic circle blazed up in lines of red-orange fire. Then he sensed a portal opening, and Master Varnart appeared within the magic circle surrounded by a glowing pool of light.

The demons pressed against the outside of the circle, the demon Eram in the lead. Their clamor was a sound like chimes and breaking crystal, and they scratched at the air above the outer circle with hands as slender and delicate as knives.

"Stand aside," Randal said to Varnart. "My friends and I need to enter your portal."

"Fool!" said Varnart. "You think drawing me here against my will has accomplished something. But I am only summoned, not bound—and if this is to be our battleground, then so be it. I am ready."

Randal's heart sank. *The spell worked—but if blood magic isn't strong enough to control a wizard with Varnart's power, then how can I hope to defeat him?*

Outside the circle, the demon Eram laughed. "Fight, mortals," he said. "And instead of the blood of one wizard, I will feast on two."

X.

Closing the Circle

"BE SILENT," Varnart said to the demon. "I'll deal with you in good time." The master wizard turned to Randal. "But first I'll have to kill you. You've gotten in my way once too often, and I don't intend to see it happen again."

"You don't dare to break the circle," said Randal. *And I don't dare use a shield-spell,* he added silently, *not until the last minute. Varnart is strong enough to break it down, just as he did the walls of Castle Doun. I'll have to wait until he makes his attack.*

"No," agreed Varnart smoothly. "I can't do anything that would break the circle." He smiled. "But I don't have to."

The master wizard gestured—and Randal felt himself being squeezed, as if an enormous hand were closing slowly on his chest and lungs. He tried to call out the words of the shield-spell, but his voice refused to answer the command of his will. He struggled in vain for breath.

Varnart stood watching him. "The trouble with

young journeymen," said the master wizard in conversational tones, "is that they forget they don't know everything. The link that brought me here still binds me to you—and the magic flows both ways."

Randal fell to his knees, and the forest darkened before his eyes. The demons outside the circle howled in delight as the circle weakened with his waning strength. Randal felt as if his bones would crack and his lungs collapse at any moment, and that would be the end of him.

With my friends dead among demons, Randal thought, as consciousness began to leave him, *and Brecelande under the hand of a false king. My nightmare showed me the truth—I've failed everyone.*

Then, through the fog that obscured his vision, he saw Lys's slender black-haired figure lunging forward to bury her javelin deep in Varnart's side with all her weight behind it.

"The trouble with master wizards," Lys snarled as she pulled the javelin out again, "is that they don't pay attention to anyone else. Walter, help me!"

Walter's greatsword was already slashing down. Varnart fell, but his spell had taken its toll. Not even the master wizard's death was enough to let Randal breathe again.

The sky seemed to be growing very dark. Randal was aware of lying on the ground—of the circle breaking—and a demon with glittering fangs floating down on graceful wings of gauze.

Then strong hands seized him by the shoulders and dragged him to the foot of the triple tree. A warm mouth settled over his, and he felt air being forced into his lungs. His sight cleared a little, and he saw that Lys was kneeling next to him. She took another deep breath and forced more air into his aching lungs.

Randal drew a long, shaky breath on his own and sat up. Lys still knelt beside him. Walter stood close at hand, his sword at the ready and his back to the threefold tree. Diamante was nearby, her fingers lightly touching the ancient axe marks on the branches of the rowan.

Randal's own hands hurt bitterly, the scar across his right palm and the new slash on his left throbbing in unison. He looked down, unable to meet his friends' eyes.

"I'm sorry," he said. "It looks like this is the end."

"It's never the end," Lys said. "Not until you're dead."

Randal looked beyond her, to the spot where the demons writhed above a shape on the ground. A bloodstained piece of embroidered velvet came loose above the snarling pack and fluttered away on the breeze.

"It won't be long," he said, pulling himself over to sit with his back to the tree. "They're distracted now, but they'll remember us soon enough."

Lys came to sit beside him, with her lute across her knees. "Can you make another circle?"

He shook his head wearily. "I haven't got the

strength for it. And besides"—he gestured toward the demons tearing at Varnart's body—"now that they've fed on a wizard's blood, what can I do to stop them?"

Lys touched the strings of her lute. The tune she played was at once sad and hopeful. Beyond her, Diamante seemed to be talking to the threefold tree, murmuring low words to it in a language that Randal couldn't understand. As she did so, the axe marks in the rowan branches began to grow over, and the pain faded away from Randal's wounded hand. The new-made gash across his left palm stopped bleeding, then closed and healed without a mark. He looked again and saw that the old scar on his right hand was gone as well, vanished as if it had never been.

He flexed his fingers, and for the first time in almost three years his hand moved freely. *Elfin magic,* he thought. *Slow but sure. If only she could have brought the same sort of healing to Brecelande. . . .*

The demon Eram detached itself from the frenzy around the fallen wizard and drifted closer to the tree. Walter followed it with his sword, point outward.

"Do not think that you can stop us," Eram said to the knight. "But if you yield, I will make your deaths painless. Offer me your throat."

"No," Walter said. "If you want our deaths, you'll have to fight for them."

The demon laughed. "Wizard's blood, royal blood, the blood of a warrior, the blood of a bard—

131

grief to the mortal world, and the Fair Realm likewise. Oh, we will have a feast indeed!"

Then, to Randal's amazement, Walter smiled. "'The Fair Realm,' you say—I thank you, Sir Demon, for the thought."

The other demons rose from their dreadful feast and began to cluster eagerly about the base of the threefold tree. Walter looked upward toward the sky of the demonic plane.

"Erlking!" the knight shouted. "Hear me! I call on you to redeem your pledge and pay your ransom! Come to me in my need!"

At that word, the demons attacked. Walter lashed out again and again. Each time he struck, a demon fell, but the severed limbs began moving on their own and crawled back to the fight.

Walter fought on. A demon grabbed the knight by his shield and pulled him forward toward the hungry mob. Lys swung her lute like a weapon, smashing it across the face of the demon that held Walter. She and Diamante dragged the knight back to the tree.

Randal pulled himself to his feet and cast a lightning bolt into the crowd of demons. A demon burst into oily black flame. The young wizard let loose another bolt of lightning, and then a sphere of white-hot fire. Two more demons went down, and Randal threw a shock-spell at a third. Since Diamante had healed the tree, he felt renewed strength and energy, but he knew that the power was draining from him with every spell he cast.

And more demons appeared. *So be it,* he thought. *If we fail here, everything is lost. From now until the end, I will use magic without regard for keeping any in reserve.*

He cast a spray of colored light that drove through demon bodies and sent them falling. Still the demons came on.

A horn blew off in the distance. It sounded long and low. A second horn joined its voice to the first, close now and coming closer.

Diamante drew a quick, delighted breath. "The horns of Elfland!" she cried out.

Then through the trees came the elfin host, green banners snapping in the wind, long swords slashing about them, and the Erlking himself riding at their head. Their lances pierced the unliving flesh of the demons, and their swords struck down their enemies. Those who fell did not rise again.

The elfin host neither stopped nor slowed their charge as they came into the clearing. The riders continued onward, and the hooves of their night-black horses broke into splinters the pile of stripped bone that marked where Varnart had fallen. The demon Eram stood for a moment in the Erlking's path, and then spun away like a leaf on the wind. The other demons broke and followed him, gibbering.

Four riderless horses galloped with the first rank of elves; red-headed Ullin held their reins. The horses halted at the foot of the threefold tree.

"Mount up," said Ullin. "You don't have all day."

They mounted. Horns sounded, and they fell in with the rest of the troop. Faster and faster they rode through the demonic forest onto a plain of bare ground. Ahead of them could be seen a spatter of green.

Onward they rode, plunging through the twilight gloom toward that spot of green. And as they drew nearer, Randal saw that it was the hill on top of which stood Castle Doun—smoke-wreathed and broken-walled, but with the High Queen's banner still flying from the watchtower.

Through the broken wall and over the rubble rode the elfin host, striking down those who still attacked the last of the defenders. The army of Hugo de la Corre scattered before the riders, for nothing could stand against their swords or the hooves of their unearthly steeds.

Riding on the air, the black horses ran up to the top of the tower; Randal and the others stopped there. Lord Alyen stood beneath his banner. Sir Palamon was beside him, and against the wall lay Master Madoc, bloodstained but alive.

The Erlking dismounted and climbed to the top of the highest parapet.

"Hear me!" he shouted, and the world fell silent. He gestured, and Diamante stepped forward beside him, as two standard-bearers held aloft the green banners of Elfland.

"This is your true queen," he shouted, and Randal knew that the sound of that voice carried to every part of the castle and field. "Does any man doubt me? Let him come forth!"

From down on the walls, a man stepped forward. He walked slowly toward the scaling ladders placed against the tower. Randal looked at him. On shield and surcoat the man bore the same black raven that had flown on the banners of the attacking army. Randal knew that this was Hugo de la Corre.

Rung by rung, Hugo climbed the ladder, and no one moved to stop him. He gained the top of the watchtower and paced across it to stand before Diamante. He towered over her. The Erlking stood behind the princess, one hand on each of her shoulders.

Hugo drew his sword from its scabbard and raised it above his head.

Once again, as in the Erlking's hall, Randal felt time slow, and then stand still. He looked at Hugo with all his senses and saw that the demon Eram was standing behind him, just as the Erlking was standing behind Diamante.

So that's the way of it, Randal thought. He raised his hand and pointed to the demon. Eram looked at Randal.

"Eram," Randal said, "I know your name. Depart. Leave men to make their own choices."

The demon looked up at him, smiled, and shook its head. Randal was suddenly furious. "Enough!" he said. "Too many mortals have already bled and died for your pleasure. Depart from this realm and trouble it no longer."

"Among my kind I am a prince," said Eram. "I do not come and go at any man's bidding."

"No," said Randal, "you do not."

As he spoke, he began in his mind the chant he had used before to open the portal between the mortal world and the demonic plane. He had no circle and no magical symbols to bind and direct the power he was calling to him—only the force of his will to see him safely through. Inside his own mind, he constructed the portal word by word and felt it take shape in the air behind Eram.

"You do not answer to every man's bidding," he said to the demon. "But now . . ."

The portal was ready. Randal summoned still more power, formed it into a lightning bolt. He held it poised.

"But now," he said, "you will answer to mine. *Aperite portae!*" he shouted. *"Ruat fulmen!"*

The lightning came down as the portal opened. A bolt of pale blue fire struck Eram in the chest and knocked the demon off its feet, sending it tumbling backward and down into the open gateway. With a long, wavering scream the demon fell, dwindled to a flyspeck, and vanished from sight.

The portal snapped shut. And time began to run forward once more.

Hugo still stood before Diamante, his sword upraised. Suddenly he knelt and turned the blade in his hand so that the hilt extended toward the princess.

"I am your man," he said. "Do with me as you will."

Diamante took the sword in her hand, balanced it for a moment, and then handed it back.

"Rise, Hugo," she said. "Take your men and go in peace." Then she added in a louder voice, so that all present could hear her, "No more will Brecelande be a place of bloodshed, but of life. So let it be done."

As she spoke, the final flare of the setting sun illuminated the top of the tower, still wreathed in smoke. A horn sounded far away over the hills. The Erlking swung back into the saddle, and the whole elfin host mounted skyward, rising higher and higher until they seemed no more than the shapes of clouds or birds. Then they were gone.

On Midsummer's Day in Brecelande, darkness came late in the evening, after long purple hours of twilight. At the coronation feast of Queen Diamante in the great hall of Castle Doun, the torches burned even later. Men and women crowded the long, high chamber, much as they had on the day that Randal came back to Doun. But this time the food was plentiful and the voices were joyous.

Diamante sat before the high table in the seat of honor. Behind her sat all the lords of the realm—Alyen, Hugo de la Corre, and Baron Ector of Wirrell among them. The baron had sustained terrible wounds during the fighting in the hall, but when the elfin host came riding into Castle Doun, he and a handful of squires and men-at-arms had still held the foot of the tower stairs.

So many folk of importance filled the high table that Randal and his friends had seats along the side of the hall at a table half-hidden in the shadows. From there, the young wizard could watch the feast and enjoy his own food in something like quiet—unlike Diamante, whose time was taken up with responding to gifts and petitions, and with accepting oaths of fealty from the numerous minor lords and nobles who had not sworn themselves to her during the coronation itself.

Lys and Walter sat on either side of Randal. Across the table sat Madoc the Wayfarer and Master Crannach. Sir Palamon stood nearby, surrounded by a group of younger knights, who looked at the master-of-arms with a mixture of respect and envy.

"Well," Sir Walter said to Master Madoc, "it looks like that prediction of yours came true. The last time you were in Doun, years ago, you told Sir Palamon that he would be in a fight that would gain him fame to the end of his days—and bards will sing about the defense of Castle Doun for that long at least."

On the far side of the hall, Randal thought he could see Master Balpesh and Mistress Pullen. He turned to Madoc and asked what the other wizards were doing there.

"Mistress Pullen no doubt is here to offer the loyalty of Tarnsberg and the Schola to the new queen," Madoc told him, "and Master Balpesh will probably also offer his friendship."

Madoc was still pale beneath his tan, for he had lost much blood from Varnart's magical arrow. But he was still alive, which could not be said of anyone else the fiery green darts had struck. Sir Iohan and many others like him had been buried on the day after the great battle.

Doun will never be the same, thought Randal. *Oh, they've mended the walls and rinsed the blood off the stones, but that can't change the past.*

He sighed. *How much of this would have happened anyway—and how much destruction did I bring here by myself?*

"What's wrong, lad?" asked Madoc. "You look like a guest at a funeral feast, not at a coronation."

"I'm sorry," said Randal. "But so many of the people I knew are gone. I don't even understand how it is that you're still alive."

Master Crannach glanced over at Madoc and smiled. "Mortal magic doesn't always work against people whose own blood isn't entirely mortal—and, you know, the women of the northern tribes sometimes take husbands from the riders in the Erlking's host."

So Master Madoc is half-elfin, Randal thought. He supposed that he ought to be surprised. But the memory came to him clearly of Madoc talking about his first meeting with the young knight who

139

would later become Diamante's mortal father: " 'So you're the son of the High King,' I said, 'and I'm the King of Elfland's second cousin.' "

Randal looked at Madoc. *I thought he was joking. But a wizard like Madoc wouldn't lie, even in jest.*

"That's fine enough," said Walter from his seat at Randal's left. "But I don't understand why, if the Erlking was able to come down to us on the demonic plane, he didn't just come through to this world and put Diamante back on the throne himself a long time ago."

"The Erlking is powerful," Master Madoc said to the knight, "and an absolute ruler in his own world. But for all his power, he cannot leave the Fair Realm—not unless someone summons him as you did, to fulfill an oath already sworn. Even though the disorder in Brecelande was causing Elfland to decay as well, he could do nothing until Randal brought you and Lys across the border into his own kingdom. Then, through the three of you, he could act and heal both realms at once."

Walter fell silent again, apparently satisfied, as a new arrival caught Randal's eye. It was Master Petrucio, a wizard from the lands to the south, far away from the rule of Brecelande. Petrucio looked about the hall and made his way quickly to where the others were seated.

"Hello, Crannach, Madoc," he said. "Am I too late?"

"Too late for supper," Madoc replied, "but I think we have a few scraps left."

"Master Petrucio," Randal said. "I thought you were Prince Vespian's man. Surely you aren't going to be swearing fealty to Diamante."

"I have a message for Her Majesty," Petrucio said. Then he smiled at Madoc and Crannach. "Just like old times, eh?"

"Master Petrucio, Crannach, and I shared a room at the Schola when we were all apprentices together," Madoc explained, in answer to Randal's puzzled expression. "They put all the outlanders in one basket. And Master Varnart was one of the young instructors who made our lives miserable."

Randal would have questioned Petrucio further, but the voice of the herald broke into the conversation.

"Sir Walter of Doun, Randal of Doun, Demoiselle Lys of Occitania—present yourselves to Her Majesty!"

Silence fell in the hall. Randal stood up and left the bench where he had been sitting. He walked forward between the rows of tables, aware of Walter and Lys walking beside him, until he came to where Diamante sat enthroned before the high table on a chair of state. There he knelt between his cousin and his friend and waited to hear the High Queen's word.

"Sir Walter," Diamante said. "Why is it that you haven't yet sworn fealty to the crown?"

"My father has already sworn fealty to Your Majesty for all of Doun," said Walter, "and I am bound by his oath."

"For Doun, yes," said Diamante. "But the kingdom of Brecelande needs an Earl Marshal to guard its borders and keep the peace. Will you swear fealty to me for that?"

Walter looked stricken. "Your Majesty, I'm not worthy."

Diamante smiled at Walter. "I need a man in that office whom I know and trust, and who better than the knight who fought for me on all three planes, at the risk of his own life? I ask you again—will you swear fealty?"

Do it, Randal urged his cousin silently. *You're as worthy as any man—and if she gives it to any one of the great lords, none of the others will trust him.*

Walter bowed his head. "Your Majesty, I do so swear."

"Then rise," said Diamante. "The safety of my life and my kingdom I give over into your keeping, and I trust you will never fail me." Walter stood and took the marshal's position, standing at Diamante's right hand. The queen turned her gaze to Lys. "Demoiselle Lys—you also have not sworn fealty."

"Your Majesty." Lys's voice was almost a whisper. "I'm a singer and an acrobat, a traveling player, and even once a thief. Kings and queens don't ask for fealty from people like me."

Diamante laughed aloud. "The King of Elfland himself called your singing worth any price you chose to name—and I say that a queen's household should be filled with music. Will you swear fealty and give your art a home in Brecelande?"

Lys's voice was even fainter this time as she answered, "Yes, Your Majesty."

"Then rise," said Diamante, "and take your place by me."

Lys stood and crossed the floor to take a bard's place, seated at the foot of the royal throne. Now only Randal remained kneeling on the floor in front of the High Queen.

Diamante said nothing, and for a long time, there was quiet in the great hall. Finally Randal himself broke the silence.

"Your Majesty," he said. "I know that I haven't sworn fealty, and I would gladly do so—but I can't. I'm still a journeyman wizard, bound to wander the known world in search of magical knowledge. My oath would be a hollow one indeed, if any moment I might be called away by the demands of the Art."

"The Art calls you now, I think," said Queen Diamante. She gestured, and from all around the hall, the master wizards came forth: Mistress Pullen, Madoc, Crannach, Petrucio, Balpesh. They all gathered around Randal.

"Do you have something to say?" Diamante asked them.

"Yes, Your Majesty," said Mistress Pullen. "We have business with this young journeyman here."

"Then carry out your work," said Diamante.

Master Balpesh stepped forward. "We have watched you carefully," he said to Randal, "from a doubtful beginning and along a difficult path to this day."

"For that reason," said Master Crannach, "just before I left Tarnsberg to come here, the Regents of the Schola voted that you should be rewarded if you—and we—lived through the battles to come."

"Prince Vespian the Magnificent, Sovereign Ruler of Peda, sends two things," Petrucio said. "First, he sends to the High Queen of Brecelande the offer of friendship between Peda and Brecelande." Then Master Petrucio turned to Randal, and the young wizard saw that he carried a bundle of folded cloth. "And Prince Vespian also sends you this, woven and stitched by the hands of the lady Blanche, whom you rescued once for no reward other than knowing that you were doing what was right."

The southern wizard unfolded the cloth that he carried. It was a robe, a full wizard's robe, with the wide sleeves and long hood of a master of the art, embroidered all over with mystic signs in silver thread. Petrucio held it open for Randal. "Come, stand up and put it on, for it is yours."

Randal was speechless. He rose to his feet and looked at Madoc for help.

"Yes, lad," said Madoc. "We know about the formal requirement to finish one's studies and present a masterpiece and all that." The northern wizard smiled. "But you haven't done a single thing the way other apprentices or journeymen do, so why start now? It's not every journeyman who can summon a master wizard like Varnart and banish a demon prince like Eram. I'd surely call that a

masterpiece. The Regents agree that the High Queen needs a master wizard by her side, and none of us could think of anyone better than you. So go on, wear the robe. You have earned it— Master Randal."

Madoc took the journeyman's robe from Randal's shoulders. Petrucio held the master's robe while Randal slipped it on, and Crannach and Mistress Pullen belted it around him.

"I ask you now, Master Randal," Diamante said. "Will you swear fealty to me, and stand by me as my court wizard?"

Randal looked from the queen to Lys at one side, then to Walter at the other. He knelt before the throne and smiled.

"With all my heart," he said.

CIRCLE OF MAGIC ❷

SECRET OF THE TOWER

by Debra Doyle and James D. Macdonald

What's a wizard without magic?

Randal broke his promise—the vow that all apprentice wizards must take never to use a weapon. Now Randal can graduate from the School of Wizardry only on one condition: that he not use magic until he is pardoned by a master wizard.

Randal must travel to the wizard's faraway tower . . . a journey made all the more perilous because he may use neither sword nor magic for protection.

When Randal finally reaches the mysterious tower, it appears to be abandoned. But he soon discovers that the building holds a deadly secret. . . .

ISBN 0-8167-6937-0

Available wherever you buy books.

CIRCLE OF MAGIC ③

THE WIZARD'S STATUE

by Debra Doyle and James D. Macdonald

Is this magic worth dying for?

Randal begins a dangerous adventure when a dying man gives him a mysterious statue. The man's last request is that Randal give the statue to a mercenary named Dagon.

Randal soon discovers that the statue possesses great power, and that Dagon is not to be trusted.

But the mercenary is not the only one who wants the statue. A warlord, a wizard, and many others in the strange walled city of Widsegard are after Randal and his friends.

What's more, the statue's power seems to be growing. Can Randal find a safe place for it, before its magic destroys him?

ISBN 0-8167-6938-9

Available wherever you buy books.

CIRCLE OF MAGIC ❹

DANGER IN THE PALACE

by Debra Doyle and James D. Macdonald

Friend or foe?

When Randal and his best friend, Lys, are invited to join the theater troupe in the court of a kind and wealthy prince, they think they have it made!

But Randal soon stumbles upon a plot against the prince and discovers that his wizardry skills are needed now more than ever.

Can Randal expose the prince's enemies before it's too late?

ISBN 0-8167-6939-7

Available wherever you buy books.

CIRCLE OF MAGIC 5

THE WIZARD'S CASTLE

by Debra Doyle and James D. Macdonald

What secrets does this fortress hold?

Bell Castle is the last place Randal wants to go. Not only is it the stronghold of his old enemy Lord Fess, but it is also shrouded in magic. Yet Randal and his friends have vowed to deliver a shipment of gold to pay the knights who have laid siege to the castle.

Soon after the companions arrive at Bell Castle, the gold vanishes—and Randal is accused of stealing it! Now he must not only prove his innocence but recover the gold as well. And that means entering the castle and defeating a wizard who has been his enemy since Randal first began to study magic . . . a wizard who has the power to trap Randal and his friends in the castle forever.

ISBN 0-8167-6996-6

Available wherever you buy books.